FRAT BOYS

FRAT BOYS
GAY EROTIC STORIES

EDITED BY
SHANE ALLISON

CLEiS
PRESS

Published in the United States by Cleis Press, Inc., 2246 Sixth Street, Berkeley, California 94710.

Printed in the United States.
Cover design: Scott Idleman/Blink
Cover photograph: Deborah Jaffe/Getty Images
Text design: Frank Wiedemann

First Edition.
10 9 8 7 6 5 4 3 2 1

Trade paper ISBN: 978-1-57344-713-3
E-book ISBN: 978-1-57344-736-2

Contents

INTRODUCTION: FRAT BOYS GONE WILD

I couldn't keep my eyes off him: his buff arms; tanned, strong legs; feet with pretty pink toes that I wanted to suck, among other things. He was the most beautiful man I had ever had the pleasure of undressing with my eyes. There he was sitting directly across from me in the lobby of the campus library. A small table strewn with his laptop and stacks of textbooks was the only thing that separated us. He was too caught up in the rapture of his reading to notice my admiration—his chiseled features; his blond, sun-bleached hair. He was like one of those guys you see on an MTV spring break special when the camera pans out to a massive audience of almost-naked, drunk college studs.

I had seen him around campus at a few events involving one of the local fraternities. As I sat there looking between his thighs, imagining him naked, my dick started to harden at such dirty thoughts. I used my book in an attempt to hide my excitement, but for me, it never takes long for things to get out of control. I tugged at it nonchalantly through my jeans, but my cock tends to have a mind of its own. It's not easy being surrounded every day by men this hot. It got so bad I stormed off to to the bathrooms on the third floor. I could feel my manhood pressing warmly against my thigh. I sidled up to one of the urinals and released my member from its cotton tomb. I had just started to take care of it when I heard the creak of the hinges from the bathroom door. It was him, the frat hunk from the library lobby. He stood at the sink, checking himself out in the mirror, finger-combing his golden locks. I stroked my dick steadily as I watched him, admiring his beauty. He soon took one of the vacant urinals next to me. We were standing so close we could have kissed. I wished we had. His sweet, pink lips pressed against mine? Hell yeah! I would have welcomed it. The frat boy undid his cargo shorts and fished out his piece. It was pretty and perfect just as I had imagined it earlier in the lobby. We stood together in silence, exchanging sideways glances. My heart was beating crazily. I gently continued to stroke myself. He quickly joined in. Damn, he was hot. I took a chance by easing my hand over and took his cock in my palm. It appeared that he was cool with how things were going down. This frat boy felt so warm and hard, his dick throbbing. He lifted his shirt up over his washboard stomach and started to play with his nipples that had a few strands of hair around them. I knew there was no time to waste. I stooped down and took him into my mouth. He tasted salty and sweaty. Just when things were getting randy, we heard someone walk in. Luckily, the bathroom was equipped with double doors so there was time for us to recover. He quickly pulled away, tucking his dick back into his baggy shorts and exiting the bathroom as a new visitor entered, completely oblivious.

Though I never saw him again after our abbreviated raunchy encounter, it's because of him that this new anthology of frat boy sex came to be. To make up for that missed frat boy connection,

I have gathered works from the best erotic scribes in the genre, to tell stories like these: A young college freshman gets more than he bargained for when he stumbles upon a hot surprise in the basement of a frat house in Hank Edwards's "Old Glory." Jeff Mann's words pulsate on the page in his tale of lust and longing between two frat brothers in "Blue Briefs." Rob Rosen will tickle your fancy and everything else in his new piece, "Big Brother." A young pledge will do anything to be accepted into a secret frat, including succumbing to the voyeuristic desires of a professor, in Gavin Atlas's "The Laius League." A pledge finds himself on the receiving end of a prank in Rachel Kramer Bussel's "Stripped." Gregory L. Norris heats it up in "The Other White Meat," while cross-dressing frat boys go wild in Z. Ferguson's, "Date Night at Delta Tau Delta." Things are romantic and sex-charged in C. C. Williams's, "The Pickup Game," and lessons don't come any harder than in Rick Archer's "Lessons from the Library." These are rounded out by steamy tales from such great erotic storytellers as Neil Plakcy, Bob Masters and Jay Starre. I hope'll you find these fraternal gatherings as erotically entertaining as I have.

Shane Allison
Tallahassee, Florida

BLUE BRIEFS

Jeff Mann

Behind the locked door, the boys are wrapped up together, naked, in twisted sheets and mid-May dawn. Their last night together is over. The light's hands slide inch by inch over their lean hips, their bushy pubes, on up past navels and smooth chests and stubbly chins. When the sun strokes Jeff's eyelids, he wakes.

Nate sleeps on as Jeff extricates himself, rises, stretches and pads barefoot to their bathroom. This room's the highest in the building, with a dormer window overlooking West Virginia University's downtown campus, the Monongahela River and the hills beyond. Jeff and Nate have been roommates—in this elegant old brick frat house; in this breezy, odd-angled room— for two years, clandestine lovers for the last year and a half. Today both sets of parents arrive for graduation; today the boys will part.

Jeff's engaged to Beverley, a pretty blonde back home in Pennsylvania, has fine job prospects, is half-relieved, half-regretful to be leaving Nate, despite the pleasure Nate's body has given him. Nate's foolish, feels too much, has gotten in too deep. Soon he'll have nothing, now that Jeff's leaving and breaking off what they have. Carefully closeted as Nate is, as he's had to be in Phi Sigma Kappa, he knows he loves Jeff, knows what kind of man that love makes him. That secret won't let him move back to his small hometown, his extended family in Barbour County, West Virginia. Instead, he's planning to relocate to San Francisco this summer, live with a distant cousin, try to become a writer, see what kind of new world he might find there.

Leaving Nate to snooze on, Jeff fetches, from the little fridge in the corner, the last can of Bud Light left. Sipping, he sits by the window, looking out over the Mountainlair Plaza, the campus buildings housing classrooms and university administration. It's a beautiful day, perfect for graduation, the leaves green-gold, the sky cloudless. A cool wind laps his unshaven chin.

But time is running out, and the May morning is not what Jeff wants most to memorize. He turns, steps over the room's clutter—packed boxes, empty beer cans, a pile of dirty clothes—and sits on the edge of the bed. He pulls the thin sheet off Nate's nakedness. He studies him, the boy he's eager to escape, the boy he wants to keep by him forever. As he studies Nate, his own cock hardens slowly, the rhythm of Jeff's heartbeat in its stiff bobbing.

Nate's snoring, funny little moans and snuffles Jeff's grown accustomed to after so many months of surreptitious sleeping together. Nate's short, only five foot six, with a tanned, stocky, muscular body. His hands are locked before him, by handcuffs he wears most nights because such restraint turns both boys on. Jeff, watching his roommate sleep, knows he loves Nate. That's why he has to leave him, to start a safer life with Beverley. Jeff sighs, stroking Nate's plump cheeks and full, bowed lips, the faint goatee framing his mouth, the shaggy brown hair already receding into a widow's peak. He strokes Nate's chest, smooth except for fur circling his nipples and a few dark curls between his pecs. He strokes his lightly hairy belly, his thickly hairy legs. He strokes his tan line, the pale skin of his hip. He suspects, rightly, that Nate's naked body will haunt him all his life.

Jeff takes a swig of beer, remembering the autumn day they met, how hard he got paddling Nate during hazing, how sweetly Nate whimpered as the oaken paddle bruised his pretty butt. Taking Nate's limp cock in his fist, Jeff strokes it, up and down, up and down.

It's Nate's turn to wake. As somber as the day will be for him, the parting from a boy he's learned to love, Nate wakes grinning, feeling the friendly, familiar pressure around his cock-shaft, the blood already stiffening him. He looks up at Jeff, rubs his eyes, stretches, folds his cuffed hands beneath his head and thrusts into Jeff's grip.

Jeff's the kind of man that has always caught Nate's eye, from his frightened adolescence in Barbour County to his first weeks on campus. Jeff's tall, six foot one, Germanic looking, with thin lips, short blond hair, angled cheekbones, several days' worth of beard-stubble. He's even more muscular than Nate, after years of gym devotion. His pale, smooth torso and arms are curved and hard, the pecs and biceps especially prominent; his long legs are shaped by jogging, coated with golden hair. Nate loves how much bigger and taller Jeff is than he, how pale and hairless Jeff's chest is, how Jeff's arms bulge when he forces Nate into assorted submissive positions. And how his blue eyes gleam, the color of morning glories, wild lobelia, horizons after a scouring rain.

The only problem's the ink, or, rather, what the ink signifies. Across Jeff's ribs is the tattoo of a stylized Christian fish. It is meant to commemorate Jesus's suffering, for it has been etched into a place a tattoo needle is likely to cause great pain. Nate doesn't want to look at it—Jeff's religious faith is one of several reasons they are not moving in together after graduation, one of several reasons they will part today—so he closes his eyes, sighs and rides Jeff's hand.

This is graduation day, so, even as Jeff grips and Nate thrusts, they're both brimful of curiosity, suspense. Where will their lives lead them? At their age, twenty-one, everything's potential. Nate's wondering if he and Jeff will ever meet again; Jeff's wondering how he can crush this sinful, dangerous and disagreeably inconvenient desire for rough sex, for short, stocky bottoms like Nate. They want to know the story before it ends; they want to know the end, like most of us. Knowledge like that might make a man feel safer—a visit to a psychic, a shuffling of Tarot cards. It might prepare us. Jeff and Nate—who knows what their futures will be?

Their creator might guess. Perhaps Jeff will get married as he plans, have three kids, make good money, settle down in a cozy suburb of Pittsburgh. Perhaps he will not be able to stop visiting interstate rest areas; perhaps he will bring crabs or much worse home to his wife. Perhaps he will end up divorced, a drunk. Perhaps he will die in his late fifties of cirrhosis of the liver. Perhaps all this will occur because he wasn't brave enough to stay with Nate.

And Nate? Perhaps, as built and hot and adorably bashful a butch bottom as he is and will be, he will find many lovers in California. Perhaps he will never find a top who satisfies him or moves him as deeply as Jeff. Perhaps he will never forget Jeff or cease to long for him, even as the agonized ache fades over the years into a wistful, regretful remembering. Perhaps, driving home from assorted teaching jobs over the next twenty

years, Nate will brood over his affair with Jeff as he listens
compulsively to country music radio, sad songs about the one
left behind, the one never recovered from, plangent voices and
minor chords and accents that remind him of the hills where he
was raised. Perhaps he will publish several poetry collections
about an intensely passionate love long ago relinquished, will
never quite find what he needs inside domesticity and the tamer
versions of lovemaking. Perhaps, one night, after two decades
of disappointing, insufficiently passionate partners, he, like Jeff,
will drink too much, will take his crotch-rocket up the tortuous
road to Mount Tamalpais, will never come back.

None of that looming unknown matters this morning, as Jeff
strokes and Nate thrusts. Now Jeff sets the beer on a side table,
checks the door to make double sure it's locked, fetches the cuff
key from his backpack, then returns to the bed, where the boys
exchange kiss after kiss, hard and deep and sloppy.

"Last time," says Jeff, as if something so momentous need
be verbalized.

Nate wants to cry; instead he nods, kissing Jeff harder.

"You want it all?" Jeff mutters as best he can with Nate's
teeth chewing his lower lip.

"You bet," Nate murmurs.

It doesn't take long for Jeff to fumble with cuffs and key, to
lock Nate's hands firmly behind his back. They've been playing
rough since the first night they made love, when, one snowy
December evening, a wrestling match led to more, Nate tied
hand and foot with bandanas, getting face-fucked on the dorm-
room floor. This lovemaking begins much the same way, Jeff
sitting on the bed's edge, Nate kneeling on the floor, mouth
stuffed full of Jeff's ridiculously big cock, a thick nine-incher,
Nate slurping and bobbing, saliva dripping off his goateed chin,
his sucking greedy and frantic, as if he knew this were his last

taste of passion, of Jeff's saline precum, as if he knew that soon he'd be starving.

Fellatio's only foreplay, though; the boys have always agreed on that. From the pile on the floor, Jeff fetches a pair of his dirty briefs. They're deep blue, like his eyes, the scanty kind that barely cover crotch and crack, the kind only a young man with a beautifully cut body can wear without looking egregious, absurd. Worn for three days in a row—Jeff's always been adverse to the tedium of doing laundry—they're rich with the musk of his butt, genitals, piss and sweat. Just the way Nate loves them: as if much of what he adores about Jeff has been distilled down into this small arrangement of fabric, like a talisman, a saint's relic, a god's cast-away. They're perfume, they're liqueur.

Nate groans with anticipation as Jeff balls up the briefs; Nate groans with pleasure as Jeff crams them in Nate's mouth. "Keep quiet; keep still," Jeff growls, the husky voice that wells up in him when he's horny, when he and Nate are alone, when Jeff's taking control. Beneath the bed's a roll of duct tape. Much of it's been used already, to secure their boxes of belongings. Some of it's used now, plastered over Nate's prettily pouty lips and cloth-crammed mouth, a strip of silver-gray extending from ear to ear, meant to keep Nate's happy noise down and restrict their long-guarded secret to the confines of this room.

Nate sinks his teeth into the blue cloth, loving the taste of Jeff's crotch and dried piss. Jeff smoothes the tape over Nate's mouth and kisses the little crease made by Nate's lips. Then, without warning, Jeff shoves Nate back on the bed, straddles him, and roughly begins kneading the smooth-skinned meat of Nate's pecs. Nate grunts and bucks beneath his lover, bliss and discomfort flickering across his face, brow furrowing, dark eyebrows wrinkling and relaxing. Soon Jeff's focusing on Nate's nipples, first with pinching fingers, then with lapping tongue, finally with nipping teeth.

When Nate starts moaning in pain, Jeff clamps a hand over his mouth, fingers digging into his jaw. It's a gesture of overpowering violence, just the thing Nate most relishes. He's helpless, he tells himself; he's a prisoner. He's been kidnapped, abducted, bound and gagged. Jeff is his captor, big-built and strong, his muscles swelling, his blue eyes gleaming and ruthless. He can and will do anything to Nate that he pleases. Nate's powerless suffering makes his cock harden even more, throbbing uncomfortably.

"Harder?" Jeff whispers. He knows exactly what Nate wants. He knows better than anyone ever will. The sex these two boys have had together for the last eighteen months is the best either will ever have. "You want it harder, don't ya?"

"Uh-huh," Nate manages to grunt beneath the weight of Jeff's hand.

"Want me to hurt 'em? Oh, yeah! You want me to hurt 'em!"

Another stifled affirmative.

"Okay, lil' dude," Jeff says, using one of the many nicknames that Nate treasures, names that, Nate hopes, might indicate how deeply Jeff feels for him. "You just be a brave boy and keep quiet now, or the guys'll hear."

With that, Jeff starts in hard, teeth burrowing into the sensitive nipple-flesh. Making love to Nate's chest has always brought out the wolf in Jeff, and soon he's growling low, tugging and twisting, just this side of bringing blood.

Such torture always leads these boys to the same place, and suddenly here they are, Nate rolled over on his belly, atop a pile of pillows, Nate chewing the makeshift gag of musky blue briefs, his legs spread, his ass in the air, his face pressed into the mattress, both boys lubed up. Jeff licks his lips, fondling Nate's butt. It's perfect, a compact, firm construction of pale curves and crack-fur. Nate's butt besots Jeff; in thirty-eight years, Nate's butt will be among Jeff's last conscious thoughts. Crazy-eager, he finger-fucks his beloved captive, a brief preparation. Nate hoists his ass higher, backing up onto Jeff's fingers, impatient, impaling himself more deeply. Now Jeff's cockhead is nudging Nate's hole—no condom, they're stupid with youth, they've barebacked from the beginning—and now Jeff shoves into him, Nate gives a little taped-up squeak, Jeff's hand once again covers Nate's mouth, and now Jeff's entirely inside and Nate's hole is burning painfully—this is the biggest cock he will ever take up his ass, and Jeff's entered him a lot faster than usual and his thrusts are violent and deep—and Nate's really hurting, but Nate suspects this might be the last time he will be filled this full, and by the very large cock of one he loves as only a boy as young as he can love, so Nate bites down on the gag, squints his moistening eyes closed, and just takes it. Soon enough, Jeff's pounding Nate's sweet spot inside, and the burning and the pain are gone, and Nate's whimpering with bliss, and Jeff's slamming home between his well-muscled little bottom's buttocks. Now Nate's bent over the bed's edge, both boys on their knees on the dorm-room carpet; Jeff's panting, one hand over Nate's mouth, the other savagely tugging Nate's tits; Jeff's snarling, "You're my bitch, Naters. Say it!" and Nate's mumbling those words into his gag, a muffled sound Jeff cherishes. Now both boys are stretched out on the floor, Jeff on top of Nate, Nate's face mashed into the carpet, his hole hammered again and again, Jeff's huge dick pushing in and out, in and out, in and out, and Jeff's slapping Nate's ass, despite the sharp sound that might alert the frat house to this sweet sodomy, and talking dirty, the way Nate savors—"You love being my bitch, don't you, Naters? You love it when I use you this way, don't you, you little whore? You love my dirty briefs crammed in your mouth, right? Don't you love this big dick up your tight lil' butt, Naters? God, oh, god, you're gonna miss being my bitch, won't you, Naters, won't you, lil' dude?"—and Nate's nodding wildly, and finally Nate's on his back, cuffed wrists beneath him chafing badly, and Nate's legs are hoisted over Jeff's shoulders. Nate's really groaning now, so Jeff's hand goes over his mouth again, but this time something feels different to Jeff, as he plows his lover for the next to last time, something feels different beneath his hand, there are not only the textures of smooth tape and stubbly cheek, but something wet, and Jeff pauses in his sweet hole-raping long enough to speak.

"You're crying?" pants Jeff. "Am I hurting you, lil' dude? Want me to stop?"

In answer, Nate cries harder, tears streaming down his face. He shakes his head, tightens his ass-muscles around Jeff's imbedded cock and squeezes, incitement to continue. Nate continues to cry, Jeff continues to ass-fuck him, increasing his pace, bending over to kiss his wet cheeks, and, three and a half minutes later, Nate's untouched cock spills over on his belly, and, five seconds after that, Jeff spills over deep in Nate's butt.

The boys lie there for a while, Nate's legs wrapped around Jeff's lean waist, Jeff slumped atop Nate. Then Jeff rises, hits the bathroom, cleans himself off, brings in a warm-wet washcloth with which he wipes up Nate's cum-moist belly and ass-crack.

Jeff tosses the cloth into the sink, then slides onto the narrow bed behind Nate. "We have two hours before the alarm goes off. You want loose?"

Nate's wrists are aching by now, his jaw sore from the packed cloth, but who knows when he'll meet another man who'll be willing to truss and gag him the way he loves, so he shakes his head and snuggles in closer to his lover. When he lifts his legs and wags his unbound feet about, Jeff takes the hint, tying Nate's crossed ankles together with a bandana before wrapping an arm around him and pulling the sheet over them. Nate weeps a little more, then drifts off, his head on Jeff's big chest. Jeff lies there, cradling his trussed lover in his arms, kissing his tanned brow, fingering his sticky ass-crack, before slipping into sleep.

The sun shifts across the room, sheeting the bed with light. The alarm goes off. Both sets of parents are due in within the hour. The boys are cuddled close, Nate's back pressed against Jeff's chest. Jeff turns off the alarm, drowsily plays with Nate's nipples. Nate's ready for more, rubbing his ass against Jeff's erection.

This is the last time they will make love. Jeff uses spit, entering Nate slowly and gently, fucking him on his side, jacking him off. Nate comes in Jeff's hand; when Nate's ass spasms with orgasm, Jeff's brought to climax and finishes yet again inside Nate.

In another two minutes, Nate's freed of ankle-bandana, wrist-cuffs, mouth-gag. Still naked, both boys stand by the bed. Nate drops to his knees and wraps his arms around Jeff's waist. "Please don't go," is what he wants to say, what the gesture says, the desperate whisper of soon-to-be-abandoned lovers from prehistory on. Neither boy can bring himself to speak. Instead, Jeff strokes Nate's hair, and Nate presses his face against Jeff's flat belly.

Jeff breaks the silence. "I'm sorry if I hurt you, lil' dude. I wanted you to remember me."

Nate can already tell that his jaw, wrists, nipples, and asshole will be aching during the graduation ceremony this afternoon, and he's glad. "You didn't hurt me," Nate says low. "And I'll remember." Bruises are the body's short-term memory, Nate thinks, and is grateful for that.

Noises in the hall. Other frat brothers are up, after another night of drinking—stumbling about, hungover, heading for showers, digging through closets, getting ready for the festivities to come. "Up, up," says Jeff, tugging Nate's elbow. Slowly, Nate gets to his feet. He feels like he's in a wind tunnel, in rushing white water. Not far ahead are the mist and the roar of the long drop.

Jeff hands Nate the handcuffs. "You better take these, Naters. I won't have any use for them. Don't want Beverley to find 'em, right?"

Nate takes the cuffs. They felt so heavy, so inescapable when they arrived in the mail, after he bought them online. His face was flushed with shame, his cock hard in his jeans, as he unwrapped the dense circles of metal. Now they feel light, incapable of restraining anyone or anything. On a whim, he locks one end of the cuffs around his left wrist, then reaches over and snaps the other end around Jeff's right wrist. Nate lifts his arm and tugs. Jeff's pulled closer. Jeff leans away, frowning. There's a knock at the door, drinking buddies making sure they're up, making sure they'll be ready for the long, hot robes, the silly mortarboards, the drive to the coliseum, the lengthy ceremony to come.

"We're up!" Jeff shouts.

"Come on, lil' dude," Jeff chides Nate, nervous. "Gimme the key."

Another knock, louder. "We're up, damn it!" Jeff shouts louder. When Nate holds up the key, Jeff snatches it. Within the minute, the cuffs are off and stashed in Nate's backpack.

The boys face each other. Jeff starts to sweat. Nate's eyes are green. Something in them makes Jeff's belly hurt. Jeff turns away, fetches the beer he left on the side table, and takes a long swig.

"Want the last?" Jeff's voice is unsteady. "Sorry; it's kinda warm."

"No." Nate's voice is strong and clear. He's staring at the fish tattooed across Jeff's ribs.

Jeff finishes the beer, crushes the aluminum can, tosses it into the wastebasket in the corner. Hurriedly, he pulls on a T-shirt, a pair of shorts, flip-flops. "Want to grab some breakfast at the Lair before the folks show up?" He can't meet Nate's eyes, the need and pain in them, the pleading.

"No," says Nate. "I'm not hungry."

"Well, you want to all have dinner tonight, after graduation? I made reservations at the Hotel Morgan. I think maybe my parents will pay for—"

"No. My dad wants to leave for Barbour County right after the ceremony, remember?"

"Yeah, right..." Jeff trails off, surveying the messy room. From the rumpled bed, he picks up the blue briefs with which he'd so recently and efficiently gagged Nate. He peels off the still attached duct tape and tosses the tape into the wastebasket. The balled-up briefs he drops into the laundry pile.

"*Shit*, we got some packing yet to do. I—I'm gonna get some coffee first," he says, brisk and abrupt, the way he always is when he feels control slipping. He unlocks the door, and there's the rest of the world waiting for him. He strides over the threshold, back into normality, and is gone. Soon Jeff will be standing in the Mountainlair, clutching his cell phone, asking his parents to pick him up there, feigning an illness that will permit him to skip graduation, to avoid the frat house till Nate and his parents are long gone, back to Barbour County. He can't face Nate; he'll never face Nate again.

Nate knows none of this, of course. He stands there for a full minute, watching frat boys in various stages of undress passing the open door. He's blinking his beautiful, long-lashed green eyes, stunned with Jeff's absence, with how fucking irretrievable things beloved can be. Then he closes the door and pulls on tattered gym shorts and a tank top. From the wastebasket, he fetches the recently finished beer can, lifts it to his lips—his lips pressed to the spot where Jeff's lips were—takes the last remaining drops in his mouth and swallows. He retrieves the strip of duct tape next, wrapping it around the beer can, where it adheres. From the laundry, he lifts his lover's blue briefs— aromatic with Jeff's body, moist from Nate's mouth. He folds them, slowly, tenderly, and slips them into a pocket of his backpack, along with the tape-wrapped can. Done, he stands by the dormer window, looking out over this college town that has seen years of his youth, months of his first, most inescapable loving. His nipples and asshole still throb from Jeff's rough use, and those dull, lingering pangs make him smile and then tear up.

In half an hour, Jeff's still gone. Nate's had another cry, cursed himself, washed his face, mustered a stoic façade and is almost done packing. He's sorting a last row of books when his cell phone rings. As he sits there by the dormer window, chatting with his mother, trying to sound as if his life isn't over but is just beginning, he feels Jeff's semen seep out of him and trickle down the back of his thigh. Something else he can't keep, he reflects. Nate hangs up, cleans himself in the bathroom, then continues his task, making two piles on the floor, one for Jeff's books, one for his own.

He's just finished when there's a knock on the door. It's his parents. He hugs his mother, shakes his father's hand. Together they load his boxes into the van. Jeff should be back by now, he thinks, but he'll see Jeff at graduation, get a chance to say good-bye. Right now, his parents are eager to grab some lunch before the ceremony, so he turns his back on the frat house and climbs into the van. *I'm young, I'm young, the best is yet to come,* he tells himself. When he cinches the seat belt around his waist and chest, he winces. Through his tank top the strap chafes his nipple, bruised and raw from Jeff's teeth.

"Mexican," he tells his parents. "For lunch...Mexican, okay? La Casa. Turn left here. Great cheese enchiladas with sour cream sauce." They bounce down the cobblestones of North High Street, beneath the hopeful green-gold canopies of spring trees, and into bright May sunlight, into what's left of the future.

BIG BROTHER

Rob Rosen

H e was the reason I pledged. Mostly. It was easy to get caught up in rush, the time fraternity row is open to the freshmen: big-ass houses, massive antebellum columns, rolling green lawns, brothers chanting, eager smiles, hearty handshakes, tales of drunken debauchery. Fuck, there were handsome young dudes lined up as far as the eye could see, a veritable ocean of them lapping at my shores. Maybe I'm stretching it a bit, but that feeling of brotherhood was tangible just as soon as you entered the houses, all of them different, but all offering the same thing. To me. Young, impressionable, *horny* me. Which is why, as I said, he was the reason I pledged.

See, during rush, they gathered us in groups, thirty at a time, to spend an hour at each house over several nights; enough time for them to get a feel for you and vice versa. But the groups quickly dwindled down after entering, smaller groups forming, brothers taking you individually to their rooms to better sell their frats to you. It happened at all the houses, sometimes

more, sometimes less. I guessed if they saw something in you
while in the smaller groups they'd likely do the whole one-on-
one thing with you. It made sense. You could tell that the nerdy
guys, the chunkier ones, the nervous-looking ones, got left in
sprawling living rooms, on back decks, in dining halls stuffed
with rows of tables. It was survival of the fittest at its most
basic.

Fine by me. Fit is good. Fit is *hot*. As was being alone with
some of these guys. Hot if not downright nerve-wracking.

This being the end of summer, the freshmen were nicely
dressed, but the frat dudes were all in shorts and tanks. It was
like a mating dance: males pushing out their chests, showing
off their plumage to better attract mates. It did the trick for me.
Him especially. Luke was tall and lean, with sinewy arms, a
smattering of chest hair poking out over the brim of his T-shirt,
nice hairy calves, even hairier thighs. He had a big mop of hair,
brown, disheveled in a *takes a good while to get it to look like
this* way; full lips, scruffy cheeks, meager soul patch, and the
most amazing eyes I'd ever taken a gander at. They were blue
like the sky on a hot summer's day, pool blue, the kind you'd
want to take a dip in. Though the tenting in my slacks meant I
wasn't standing up to do any dipping any time soon.

Long story short, we hit it off immediately. We had both
played high school baseball, had the same small-town roots;
both only children, good students, with a penchant for comic
books. My ears were ringing; my dick was hearing *blah, blah,
blah* and screaming for release. Not that sitting in a guy's room
during rush is a good time for picking someone up, mind you,
but it's a start.

A week later, they asked me to pledge. Well, Luke asked me,
with several of his brothers nodding and smiling behind him.
Not that I saw any of them, though. Just him. Tunnel vision. I

said yes, my voice all squeaky, legs trembling, the now-familiar tent in my slacks.

I loved fraternity life right away, loved the whole mentality of it, the *all for one and one for all*. I enjoyed the partying, the hazing, the group camaraderie; watching games on the jumbo TV, sprawled out, surrounded by hot guys, all cussing and cheering and fist pumping, thick mounds of underarm hair visible from minute to minute. And there was Luke, right next to me or nearby, always with a pat on the back, a punch to the arm, a sly grin, with his perfect teeth, and those perfect eyes lit up in dazzling blue.

At the end of the year, I went from pledge to brother. It involved the usual hush-hush secret rites: the things you read about and see in the movies. That same fateful day they assigned me a big brother, someone to guide me. Luke. As if my dick hadn't gone through enough already; poor, throbbing, aching peter. Still, I was happy. It felt right: I had a big brother at last.

And that should've been enough. But there was to be icing on that cake.

Next year, I moved into the house. There were forty individual cramped rooms, mostly messy, beer-strewn and bong-cluttered. Mine was no exception. And it was right next to his, as I soon found out. He greeted me the week before school started, beer can in his outstretched hand, megawatt grin, sparkling eyes: a great way to start the semester.

The party that night was loud, beer-soaked and celebratory; eighty brothers, all glad to be back together again. Music was blaring, fraternity chants were hollered; girls were coming and going, horny brothers wobbling on drunken legs, bleary-eyed. I skipped the girls, of course, opting for the keg and the company of friends, Luke was at my side, matching me chug for chug. Hours later, blitzed and tired, I weaved my way back to my room, shutting the noise of the festivities out as I closed the door behind me before falling into my futon. Only, a buzz of sound soon permeated my haze.

'Twas the sound of sex.

And it was coming from next door. Adrenaline quickly cleared the booze fog, my rising cock leading the way to the wall that separated us. With ear against wood, I eagerly listened in, dropping my shorts and boxers a quick second later, my prick getting a furious pounding just after that. If I couldn't have sex with Luke, at least I could secondhandedly do so.

Only, it wasn't Luke having sex. You could tell right away it was a video; too much pausing and fast-forwarding to be the real deal. Still, it meant that Luke was next door, just as naked as me, just as hard, yanking the come up from his balls. I groaned at the mere thought of it, the image filling my head in brilliant Technicolor. Still, something wasn't right. The sound was too crisp, not muffled enough. Not that I was complaining.

I moved my ear an inch away and listened intently: I found the source. There was a hole in the wood siding, just beneath the desk that was built into the wall, impossible to see unless you were looking for it.

Butt naked, I crouched down and got on all fours. It looked like a mouse hole, tiny and poked out, maybe an inch wide, gnawed all the way through. By putting my eye to the wall, I could see into Luke's room, just below his desk; could watch Luke as he pounded his meat, his back against the rear of his futon as he watched the video that now splashed across his TV screen.

And let me tell you, his meat gave a whole new meaning to the term "big brother."

I'd only ever seen Luke shirtless before, his torso etched with tiny muscles, a coating of wiry fuzz on his dense pecs that funneled down to a six-pack with two extra cans. Now I had the full picture. And, man, was my cock ever happy—as was Luke's, as he slowly tugged and stroked and yanked and pulled on that thick slab of his, eight steely inches of pink flesh, the head as big as a plum, bouncing balls the size of lemons. His other hand was fiddling with the remote, stopping and starting the action on the screen, his fist moving rapidly when he found what he liked. Mine was moving hummingbird-fast now, aiming my cock at the carpet for the inevitable, which came just as he did.

With his legs bouncing and his head tilted back, that giant cock of his erupted like Vesuvius, a thick gush of molten-hot come spewing up and out, followed by several smaller bursts. White magma dripped down his heavily veined shaft, his moans and groans reaching my ear before trembling down my body, causing my cock to shoot streams of come that landed on the carpet, all while my eye remained glued to that precious hole.

And then it was glued to Luke, as he stood, that fifth limb of his gloriously jutting out and swaying as he wiped himself off then flicked off the lights and crashed, as it sounded to me, on his futon. I fell into mine, my mind replaying the scene over and over again as I drifted off to sleep.

The next morning I came out of the shower—sadly we had private ones—just as he was going in. I caught sight of his stunning ass as his towel got hung on the hook, my own towel quickly wrapped around my midsection in the nick of time, before my cock went instantly rigid. Trying to steady my breathing, I walked back to my room. His door was ajar. I looked down the hall and found myself alone, so I sneaked inside.

First I sniffed the floor, where vestiges of moisture and the smell of spunk were still evident, causing my cock to pulse and beg for freedom. Next I turned and spotted his stash of videos beneath the TV. I groaned at the covers, which showed big-titted women getting boned by huge-dicked dudes. Luke, it seemed, had a penchant for bodacious knockers. I had my own penchant, and he was still down the hall scrubbing it up. Mine, naturally, was begging for release, which it got, quickly, but next door.

After that, the hole got checked out on a regular basis. Being right next door to Luke, I knew where he was or wasn't most of the time. I knew when he was alone in his room. The first couple of days I caught sight of him naked or nearly naked quite a lot, his fine, lean body standing or sitting, stretching out, working out, sleeping. My big brother, needless to say, became an obsession, one taken way over the edge three nights after my fortuitous discovery.

It was late. Most of the guys were out at a nearby pub. Luke and I, opting to stay in, had just finished watching a game and I had gone back to my room to catch some sleep, but, of course, I checked on the hole first. I sucked in my breath, my eye going wide and my cock instantly stiff inside my shorts. Luke was sitting at his desk on the other side of the hole, naked and hard, that massive, stunning cock of his barely two feet away. A translucent bead of precome was slicking up the wide, helmeted head, and his rod was pointing my way, unattended while he typed away on his keyboard, everything above his finely etched belly out of sight.

Within seconds, I was naked, my cock lubed up with spit and a slow, even stroke begun; my face was pressed up tight to the wall, watching, waiting. Soon enough, I guess he found what he was looking for on his laptop, because his hand was reaching down for a grip and a tug, the only sound that of his chair groaning as he shifted his weight, his legs spread wide, leaning back as he pumped away, heavy balls grinding into the leather. *Lucky leather.* Lucky me, too, to have such a bird's-eye view, so up close and personal like.

Then again, maybe not so lucky.

The carpet was dusty. The sneeze came out before I could stop it.

I froze. The scene unfolded in slow motion. Luke jumped, cock swaying to and fro as he tumbled from his chair. It didn't take him long to spot the source of the sneeze, the hole beneath his desk. I watched as those dazzling eyes of his zoomed in, becoming one on the other side of the wall. I jumped back, cock still in my hand, fear riding shotgun down my spine. I heard the stomping of his feet, the flinging open of his door, the pounding on mine, all in mere seconds. Terrified, and rightly so, I wrapped a towel over my dwindling cock and pried open the door.

"What the fuck?" he yelled, pushing his way inside.

I quickly closed the door behind him, in case there were any brothers still in the house. Not that I would be part of the fraternity very much longer, I gathered by the look of rage on Luke's otherwise stunning face. "I heard a noise and spotted the hole," I tried, squelching a sob. "I bent down the same time you did."

"Bullshit!" he yelled, trembling now. "You made the hole to watch me."

I shook my head. "No, dude. It was there when I moved in. Probably a mouse."

He inched in closer, index finger poking at my rapidly expanding and contracting chest. "Then why were you naked." He paused. "And, um, and hard?"

I backed away, tripped, fell, staring up at him now. "Doing the same as you, dude. Just a coincidence."

"Bullshit," he said again, a flush of red splashing across both stubbled cheeks. "Bullshit." He sounded less sure this time.

I gulped, my back up against my futon now. "Sorry, dude. Really. It was an accident. Let's just forget about it." I tried a smile. "We're brothers. You're my big brother." He gripped his towel, sighed, clearly unsure of what to do next. "Come on, I'll do anything. Let's just drop it." I looked around the room, hoping a solution would present itself. Amazingly, my salvation hung from a hook on the wall. My pledge paddle, given for show—until now.

He followed my gaze, shaking his head, but moved over to it just the same. He took it down and smacked it against his palm. "Take the towel off, Ron," he said, with a grimace.

I held on to it, tightly. "Aw, come on, Luke," I stammered, my voice barely above a whisper.

"Off," he said, through gritted teeth, eyes mere slits now. "And bend over the futon."

Even as a pledge this had never happened to me. Still, he meant business. Perhaps this was the only way out of the mess I now found myself in. I released my grip on the towel and dropped it to the floor, all while he smacked the paddle against his palm. Then I turned, my chest on the seat of the futon, face against the back, knees on the carpet, ass out, cock and balls dangling. "It was an accident, dude," I tried again.

He moved in, directly behind me. "Bullshit," he repeated, bringing the wood up flush to my ass before patting me with it, a light *thwack* that caused me to flinch. He brought the paddle back and let it swing, harder this time; my face was buried in the futon, which barely muffled my groan. He got on his knees for the next smack, sending the wood flying against my tender flesh. Then he did it again. "You like that, Ron?" he asked, all sinister like, a wicked edge to his voice. "You like to be humiliated? Watched?" Another smack, then another, my cock stiff, pressed up against the edge of the futon. "Huh, Ron? Tell me you like it."

I cursed beneath my breath. "No fucking way," I spat, eyes shut tight.

"No?" he asked, nearly breathless. "Come on; tell me you like getting your ass beat, Ron."

Smack. Smack. My cock was ready to burst. "Fine," I grunted. "I like getting my ass beat. Now quit it."

He grabbed my shoulder and flipped me around, suddenly, so we were face-to-face, those spectacular blue eyes looking down at my throbbing, swaying cock. "Yeah," he rasped. "I can see how much you like it."

Mine wasn't the only raging boner in the room. His towel was tenting something fierce. When I looked back up, his eyes were locked with mine. It was then that the lightbulb went off over my head. "Those videos you watch," I said, his face so close to mine that I could smell his breath as he huffed and puffed. "It isn't the big tits you like, it's the big dicks." He paused, his face expressionless, then the slightest of smiles appeared. I continued. "You got me this room, Luke. You arranged it." In a flash, my hand reached out, gripping his massive tool, his eyelids fluttering upon contact. "*You* put that hole down there."

The smile traveled northward. "That's what big brothers are for, Ron," he whispered, leaning in, his lips brushing mine. "By the way, you sure do jack off a lot."

I slapped his chest with my free hand, stroking him through the towel with the other one. "Fucker. You set me up."

He reached in and grabbed a hold of my cock. "Speaking of *up*." He gave it a tug, and a thick bead of precome oozed up and over. And then he leaned in again, his kiss hard, insistent, our tongues thrashing, our faces quickly spit-soaked. Then he broke away, a wide grin plastered to his face. "Sorry, little brother; I had to make sure. This, um, well, *this* isn't exactly kosher in a frat house."

He had a point. "You could've just asked me and saved my ass that beating."

He laughed. "Really? Could I have?"

I shrugged. "Guess not. But you owe me one." I kissed him again, softer this time, my body melting into his, his heart thumping against my chest, hands roaming my backside.

"How about you play with a different hole of mine then?" he offered. "Will that make us even?"

"It's a start," I replied, watching eagerly as he turned around and got on all fours, towel dropped, boulder-sized balls dangling low, heavy cock even lower, all beautifully framed in alabaster, his pink hole winking out at me, hair rimmed, delicious looking. I hungrily dove in, falling to my knees and burying my face in all that beautiful flesh. I lapped him up, sucking around his crinkled portal, parting him with my tongue, shoving it in.

He moaned, rocking his ass into my face, reaching around to pull his cheeks apart for me. I breathed in deeply, inhaling the musk of him while tugging on his nuts. "Fuuuck," he purred, the sound traveling down his body and into mine, causing every one of my nerve endings to shoot off fireworks.

I crawled on my knees to his side, cupping his chin in my hand before leaning down to kiss him again. My other hand went in the opposite direction, two fingers smacking at his slicked-up chute, two fingers gliding in, just the tips, then out, in again, deeper, all while I made out with him. He moaned, pushing his exhale into my lungs.

He reached between his legs and stroked his giant cock. I did the same with mine, while I finger-fucked his tight ass. "Come with me, dude," he groaned into my mouth.

I chuckled. "Never thought I'd hear those words," I said, mashing my mouth into his, slamming my fingers all the way inside of him, cramming them down to his farthest reaches. And then my cock pulsed, just before shooting massive bursts that hit his side over and over again. His body quaked, back trembling, both of us panting as he shot next, his moans mixing with my groans, my spunk sliding off him, the aroma of come all-enveloping, the sound of our sex bouncing off the walls around us.

He collapsed, my fingers popping out of his ass. I rolled him over, his cock still full, dripping with come. So beautiful, Michelangelo couldn't have done better. I slid in next to him, tweaking his eraser-tipped nipples as we both fought to catch our breaths.

He ran his fingers across my lower back, tickling the hairs above my crack. Then he turned his face to mine, smiling brightly, those eyes sparkling like sapphires. "Hey there, little brother," he whispered.

I smiled back at him, my hand roaming his muscled torso. "Hey there, big brother."

He laughed. "Kind of sounds fucked up, huh?"

"Kind of."

He paused, face leaning in so he could kiss my forehead. "But I like it."

I shut my eyes and nestled my face into the crook of his neck. "Me, too, Luke," I said, with a slight nod of my head. "But no more straight porn, okay? Those big titties scare me something fierce."

"No problem," he replied. "Besides, I got me all the big dick I need right here."

I stroked my dick, the thick flesh already growing thicker in my grip. "Amen, big brother," I said, slapping it against his hairy thigh. "Amen to that."

DATE NIGHT AT DELTA TAU DELTA

Z. Ferguson

Kyle and I were standing outside the Sigma Nu fraternity wearing garbage. Not bad clothing, real garbage: banana peels, wet tissues, potato peelings, half-eaten sandwiches. At least they were all recyclables. It was getting cold, but we dared not speak. "Garbage doesn't talk without permission," said Delta president Keith. "Insolent garbage doesn't get admitted to Delta Tau Delta, the most exclusive frat on campus."

"Garbage, you may speak," said Keith the Rush president, looking at our refuse-strewn bodies.

"May we come inside?" asked Kyle, who was shivering, his penis retracted to almost nothing. Mine was not far behind.

"Garbage, you have a choice. You can come inside and take your rightful place in the kitchen wastebaskets, or you may prepare for Date Night.

We looked at each other. That's a choice? How bad could Date Night be? We'd probably be forced to date the ugliest girls in the neighboring Tau Epsilon sorority house, maybe give them oral sex? Kyle nodded to me and we answered, "Date Night."

"Date Night it is!" said Keith, a little too enthusiastic for our comfort. "Kyle and Mark come in and be prepared for your dates."

We were hustled in through the Delts lining the stairs and cheering, and up to the showers, where four frat brothers awaited with shaving cream cans and disposable razors. We were put under the showers and the cold water was turned on. Cold as it was it was better than standing outside. Then came the warm, then hot. I felt myself almost relaxing, then Keith called out, "You must get ready for your dates. It is important for you to look your best. You represent DTD and all that that entails. Brothers, shave them."

They set up on us, turning our backs to the crowd and lathering up our bodies. Someone was getting a bit too into this—I felt soapy fingers up between my buttcheeks, poking my hole. As we were being turned around, other hands ran between my legs, fingering my ass and cupping my balls. My manipulators looked into my eyes. I saw nothing but churlish delight. The bastards knew what they were doing. My cock was reacting. Kyle, who was shorter than me, a thin marathoner, was jerking away from the hands, but his dick, too, was in a semi state and rising.

"Brother Kyle, you must submit. This is Date Night."

If Kyle hadn't been cursed with a competitive streak, he might have quit right then, but we both wanted to be in Delta House more than anything. It was said the connections alone guaranteed good grades, an easy ride through college, dates with sorority chicks and a great job after graduation. Deep down inside, I knew Kyle wanted to belong more than me and probably was hoping I would drop out or not get accepted. I felt the army of razors shaving our backs and legs. There was hair all over the shower floor, as razors removed hair that no man alone could reach. Then they turned us around again and shaved our pubes and under our balls. Thank god these guys had done this before. Again there was quite a bit of manipulating, and I was jutting hard. A cloud of *whoos* rose in the room as the guys watched.

"Pledge dicks, pledge dicks, harder, harder," they cried.

"Keep those cocks hard, Pledges, so we can shave those rods clean." Both of us were sticking out and up, trying to hold still. After we were shorn, Pledge President Keith grabbed my dick and started stroking, while having me sing the house song. I sang out loud, while Kyle, his cock hard and bouncing, watched me get jacked off. Keith had a way with hard dicks, and soon I just cried out as I came to the applause of the house members. Kyle was next, and Keith applied a strategic finger to his ass, while stroking. Kyle tried to sing, but surrendered to the feeling and shot three streams of come almost four feet. The brothers exploded in cheers. Keith brought them to attention.

"Brothers. Enough. You must retire to the living room downstairs and await your dates. Mark"—that was me—"this way with Chuck; Kyle, go with Wendon. Hurry, hurry Pledges, you must get dressed. It's Date Night."

Chuck led me into a bedroom and there on the bed was my outfit: skirt, blouse, shoes, bra, wig—and at the mirrored table was makeup.

"You're kidding..."

"Pledge, get those clothes on, right now."

Fuck. I looked at the ensemble. I was five ten and one hundred and sixty-nine pounds, a former wrestler and rugby player. I looked at Chuck.

"Come on..."

"Look, Pledge, you wanna be a Delt or not? You gotta do this. It's only for a night." Chuck pulled me in close. "I get punished if you back out, and Keith's like Mr. Sadist. Come on." I looked at Chuck's eyes. They were watering, so I nodded and picked up the skirt.

"Where's the underwear?"

"No underwear."

"No panties...Jesus."

I slipped on the skirt and looked at it in the mirror. It was short, and when I bent over, my butt popped into view. Chuck handed me what looked like a couple of flesh-colored water balloons.

"These go on your chest, then the bra goes on. Hurry up. I still have to do your makeup."

Makeup. It turned out Chuck and Wendon were theater majors. I sat in the chair as Chuck transformed my face into a woman's, complete with fake eyelashes, the whole time giving me hints and directions on how to do it myself.

"No Botox injections?"

"Don't get cute, Mark. Get your shoes on."

I didn't get nylons.

I stood and looked at myself in the mirror. It was kind of incredible. I wore a dark wig reminiscent of Katie Holmes and plaid skirt of the private school porn variety, with a white blouse, of course. My socks were white; my shoes, black flats. Someone paid attention to the latest fashion. Downstairs, I could hear the thunder of the guys pounding the tables and stomping their feet. I turned sideways and back. Chuck handed me my makeup bag.

"You have to keep yourself made up all night. And don't sit next to Steve, who's head of the pledge committee or Lonnie, the sergeant at arms, whatever you do. Okay. Ready?"

I exhaled. "Yeah, I guess."

"You look great, by the way. And camp it up, otherwise, you'll get bounced."

"Thanks. I think."

I walked down the hallway hearing, "Katie, Katie, Katie." I guess that was my name for Date Night. I got to the stairs, daintily grabbed the banister and descended into hell as the house erupted in cheers and screams. Guys were on the landing, flipping up my skirt and smacking me on my bare ass. The skirt was light. I could feel my cock nodding underneath it. A guy grabbed me and gave me a kiss, another slipped his hand around my waist, and whispered, "Baby" as he lifted my skirt, and went for my cock. I pushed him away and yelled, "Fresh bastard." The place erupted in cheers. But where was Kyle?

"Pledge, you are beautiful," said Keith, "and don't mind the coarser members of the house." I looked around for Kyle, as the group started to chant "Madonna, Madonna, Madonna." Then Kyle appeared at the top of the stairs, and I nearly shit.

Kyle was decked out in complete Madonna gear circa 1980, with black nylons, garter belts and black bustier and a short black skirt. It was an improvised outfit, as Madonna didn't wear a skirt, but the makeup was accurate right down to the smoky eyes. The wig was perfect. I stared as "Vogue" played while Kyle descended, in rhythmic, languid steps. No one touched him. The music played and Kyle aka Madonna touched foot to the bottom step, sashayed over to me, then stood gyrating his hips. The place shook in cheers and chants of "Lez kiss, lez kiss, lez kiss."

Kyle grabbed my chin and planted one square on my lips as camera flashes went off all over the room. I stood shocked and awed at Kyle's over-the-top portrayal. Keith dove in and quieted the crowd.

"All right, I guess we know which pledge is the sexiest..." The crowd hooted and yelled. Kyle was breathing hard, giving the boys the Queen's wave.

"Okay, ladies, we have to get going. You have your makeup bags?"

We looked at each other.

"Where are we going? No one said anything about *going anywhere*," I said, hands on my hips.

"Out on our date, of course. We have to go to Hillers Ale House."

"Fuck," said Kyle under his breath. I stood flummoxed, wondering how this was going to play.

"Ladies, now go fix your makeup and we'll bring the car around. Guys, we're off to Hillers!" A big roar went up, as Kyle and I went to the restroom to redo our lipsticks and such. Once inside, I closed the door and checked the stalls to make sure no one was inside with us. I confronted Kyle.

"Where did that kiss come from?"

"Mark, dude, I had to make it realistic."

I stood at the mirror reapplying my lipstick.

"Well, knock it off."

Kyle stood next to me, checking his skin toner and mascara. I recounted my trip down the stairs.

"Who's the guy with the wandering hands? I couldn't keep him off my ass. And what's with the rubbing his crotch on me? He has a big dick, too. I felt it in the crack of my butt. Asshole."

Kyle nodded. "Yeah, this one guy got me at the top of the stairs. Lifted up my skirt and grabbed my cock. Apparently it was not enough to jack us off in the shower. I'm beginning to think this is a frat full of homos."

"I know what you mean," I said.

"But can I tell you something?" Kyle said in a low voice, smiling.

I touched myself and chuckled. "I know what you're gonna say. All this attention is making me horny, too."

He lifted up the front of his skirt to show me his hard-on, then pointed at me. "Come on, dude, let's see yours…"

I blushed. "It's all the excitement, I guess, and the touching. I didn't know my ass was an erogenous zone." I lifted my skirt to reveal my bobbing boner. Kyle grabbed his and started stroking.

"Keep your skirt up, Mark, lemme look. I gotta get off, before I go back out there."

"Jesus, Kyle, friggin' pervert… Okay, hurry it up. Oh shit… Wait. Lemme stroke with you."

We turned to the mirror and stroked our hard dicks while holding up our skirts.

Kyle and I first beat off together long ago, at a sleepover, when we were in our early teens. We dared each other to run around naked outside and then did it, and when we got back to the tent, we were both breathing hard and our dicks were stiff as boards. I tried rubbing it out on the sleeping bag, but it was hopeless. Kyle, always the showman, just rolled onto his back and grabbed his dick.

"Come on, dude," he said, "show me yours…"

I lay on my back and we both hit it until we came. We slept well that night. We kept that evening a secret between us, but not without the occasional return bouts.

Looking at Kyle now as Madonna, with his thick hard prick sliding in his hands and the look of lust on his made-up face, I came in an instant; then Kyle, seeing me, exploded, his come hitting the mirror.

Someone was banging on the bathroom door.

"Hurry up, you lezzies. What are you doin' in there? Hurry up."

I looked at the splooge on the mirror and grabbed a tissue.

"Fuck, Kyle you didn't have to drown the mirror..."

"Hey, like I can control it. Now I have to do my makeup all over again. I'm all sweaty. No thanks to you."

Hillers Ale House is a big place with pool tables, foosball and pinball machines. There's a dining room, and if you drink beer, the bar is a sight to behold, with hundreds of independent labels on tap and in bottles. The munchies are top-notch, and the servers are gorgeous. Kyle and I practically lived there, illegally, our sophomore year.

We sat in the backseat with a couple of other gropers, dreading the arrival. I managed to sit next to the notorious Lonnie, who kept making all sorts of rude comments like, "If you were a chick, man, I'd bend you good," and, "How much for a blow job?" His hand, though not touching my cock, hung between my legs, and his fingers managed to bump my junk every time we stopped at a stoplight or hit a pothole. By the time we got to Hillers, I was hard as a rock from all that indirect contact. He gave me leering glances.

"You want it, don't you, bitch?" he said, and laughed as he got out, but not before giving my hard-on another squeeze. Kyle didn't fare much better. Apparently, the notorious Steve thought Kyle really *was* Madonna, and kept blowing in his ear and rubbing his thighs.

"Come on, baby, let's have a peek," he said, opening Kyle's legs. He kept kissing his neck and Kyle was getting pissed. And hot. A guy in the front seat turned around and looked between Kyle's legs at his stiffy.

"Ooh, Madonna's got a hard one tonight..."

They all watched as we struggled out of the car, legs open, and dangles swinging to their applause and laughter. We adjusted ourselves and our dates took our hands and led us in the door.

As messed up as the evening was, going to Hillers was a relief. Hillers was a total college place, and so much outrageous stuff from frats has occurred there in the past, a bunch of guys, two of whom are dressed as female celebs, barely raised eyebrows. This was the place that held a naked pool tournament, last year.

Hillers was packed. There were lots of wait staff, carrying trays of pitchers, under the boom of rock, disco and hip-hop; everything from Rolling Stones to Young MC, from Santana, to Kyle's consternation, Madonna.

Steve ran a hand under Kyle's skirt.

"They're playing your song, babe."

Kyle slapped his hand, but it had done its damage. Kyle could feel the head of his dick grazing his skirt. And the crowd that night wasn't helping. It was Ladies' Night.

I walked in arm and arm with Lonnie, who suddenly seemed to forget we were on a date and immediately honed in on the beer. We got a table, and he and Steve started drinking, which was fine with us. We scoped out the women.

"We are definitely coming back as guys," said Kyle, "Mark, check this out." He flipped up his skirt to show me his dick; hard and almost crimson at the head. I opened my legs, also, and mine quivered in the thick warm air.

"Jesus, man," Kyle said, snickering, "we need to get to the can and take care of these. We're in danger of coming out. Like out from under our skirts."

"Okay, Kyle, which can?"

We looked at each other, then burst out laughing. A couple of girls came over.

"You guys look great. Your friends told us about you two."

"We're not what you think," Kyle said, "It's a frat thing."

They sat at our tables. "I think you lost your dates," they said, pointing to the foosball table. Lonnie and Steve were in deep competition, slamming both the table and the beers.

"I'm Rachel and my friend's Jennifer."

"I'm Kyle, aka Madonna, and Katie here, is Mark."

They chuckled. "You guys and dolls wanna dance?"

We looked at each other. Then rose.

The dance floor was small, packed and effective as we moved to Earth Wind and Fire's "Sing a Song," a fine retro groove. Jennifer and Rachel were witty, bouncy fun, a couple of girls with whom, if the situation had been different, we would've headed home much earlier. Kyle's a better dancer than me, but that night I felt pretty damn free and for a moment, we let go of the fact that we were dressed like chicks, except for Jennifer, who kept trying to reach under my skirt. They were surreptitious attempts, granted, those occasional passes of the hand as she spun that seemed to be in the right place just as my skirt flipped up. Rachel gave up trying to be subtle with Kyle, and during Gnarls Barkley's "Crazy," managed to get behind him and give him a bold reach-around. Kyle and I were in erection heaven, these being our first female hands in quite a while.

But it was too good to last. When we returned to our tables, cocks bobbing, horny as hell, kissing our girls in desperate, furtive moments, there sat Lonnie and Steve, drunk and pissed.

"What you guys doin? You're *our* dates, bitches," said Lonnie. The two girls, not wanting to get in the middle, smiled weakly and eased away.

"Hey," I said to Steve, "where's your manners?"

Kyle watched them depart and said nothing, but I could tell he was pissed.

"We gotta go home," said Steve, slapping the keys on the table. "Home, girls."

They stood, and I decided to be the designated driver. They draped themselves over our shoulders and we four eased through the crowd and out to the parking lot, where Lonnie let loose a puke that I hadn't thought was possible from a guy. Steve followed suit, and we stood watching our men spray paint the concrete.

"What are you bitches lookin' at?" yelled Lonnie. "Start the fuckin' car."

"What about the other guys?"

"Don't worry about them, Katie, just get in. Delts can survive."

"Yeah! Delt's rule," screamed Steve piling into the backseat and grabbing Kyle.

Kyle tried to move up front with me and Lonnie, but Steve got pissed.

"You think you're better than me? Get back here..." His head fell back and all the way home it was, "How about a blow job...you owe me a blow job, Madonna...blow job..."

Lonnie was pretty cautious with me. Even though his hand was sliding up my thigh, I was able to keep him in line by threatening to drive us all into a guard rail.

We made it back to the house and got the guys upstairs, both of us slinging our dates onto their beds like they were large empty kegs. Lonnie was passed out for the night, so I went in to help Kyle with Steve, who was getting randy and aggressive.

"Lemme see under your skirt, baby...Lemme see..." Steve grabbed Kyle's skirt, lifted and clutched at his cock, pulling on it. Kyle looked at me.

I grabbed Steve's hand and tried to break it free but Steve gripped harder. Kyle winced.

"Give me that dick..."

The air seemed to grow thick with silence, and the night

swerved into ugly territory as Kyle stood at the side of the bed, closer to Steve, who pulled Kyle's dick to his mouth. Kyle looked at me, bit his lip and put one knee on the bed, bringing his hardening cock closer to Steve's lips.

"Kyle, it's not worth it, man...."

Kyle shot me a Cheshire grin.

"Hey, if he wants it..."

He lowered his hips and Steve took the length of Kyle into his mouth and sucked and licked like Kyle's dick was a cherry Popsicle. I watched, my own cock getting hard as the noise of Steve's oral work filled the room. Kyle started moving his hips. Steve held Kyle's balls then reached through his legs and fingered his ass. Kyle gasped, pulled off the skirt, and succumbed. He looked at me, muttering, "Jesus, Mark...he's good...fuck... I'm...oh, man!"

Steve raised his head and continued his wild work on Kyle's dong. I couldn't watch much longer without lifting my skirt and stroking to their sex play. Then Steve let go of Kyle's prick, unsnapped his pants and wrestled them down his legs.

"Mark, I want you to fuck me. Come on, Katie...fuck me..."

I looked at Kyle but he was in another world, stroking his cock that was hot and wet from Steve's lips. Steve raised his ass and spread his legs.

"You want in? You want to be a Delt?" I took off my skirt, kicked off my shoes, climbed onto the bed and eased my cock into Steve. He groaned like a squeaky door, as I pulled out and stuck him again, going deep.

"Condoms are in the drawer," mumbled Steve between sucks, but it was too late for that. I was about to come, and Kyle had already shot his wad onto Steve's face and chest. I humped him hard, then felt my come surge through me and into Steve.

Kyle and I got off Steve, and Kyle smoothed down his skirt. My wig was wet with sweat, my chest bare and plastic boob-free, but Kyle still looked hot—probably what Madonna looked like after plunging a strap-on into one of her favored dancers in her hotel room after a concert.

Steve rolled onto his back, looking at the ceiling. The effects of the beer were probably waning. He raised his head and looked at us, two pledges who had just fucked his ass well.

"Now, get out of here," he said in a whisper.

We didn't get pledged. As we left the meeting the next day, we noticed a pile of women's clothing dripping from the Dumpster, atop empty cases of beer and other junk. No one had said anything to us. Neither Steve nor Lonnie even showed. Kyle and I remained silent until we left Greek Row. Kyle looked at me.

"You got mascara on your left eye, still," he said. I wiped my eye with my sleeve.

"So what you want to do, now?" I asked him.

"I could use a beer at Hillers."

"Cool."

OLD GLORY

Hank Edwards

I had known Jessie since freshman year in high school and was glad she had decided to attend the same college I chose. We had been attending classes for two weeks now and I had developed a crush on a guy in my biology class: Kevin Sanderson. He was tall and lean with dark, wavy hair and dark eyes. I didn't think he was gay, but we had struck up a few conversations and his voice had a habit of staying with me the rest of the day. I met up with Jessie one afternoon at the student union where she sat in the smoking section.

"We are going to the party this weekend, right?" Jessie asked.

I dropped my book bag on the floor next to me and cocked my head. "Party?"

"The Omega rush party." She looked around before leaning over the cafeteria table and lowering her voice. "I hear they have a glory hole in the basement."

I swallowed past a dry lump in my throat. "Glory hole?"

She narrowed her eyes. "You don't know what a glory hole is?"

I felt myself blush and dropped my gaze. "Of course I do."

"What is it?" she challenged.

"A hole cut in the wall of a bathroom stall," I replied. "For oral sex."

She made an impressed face. "Okay, maybe you've seen a movie or two."

I thought fleetingly of the porn DVDs I had hidden away in my dorm room. I did enjoy a glory hole scene with a wet, sticky ending, but I pushed those thoughts out of my mind and asked, "So the Omega house has a bathroom stall in its basement?"

"Not exactly. Rumor has it the guys have an old shower stall set up in the middle of the basement. There's a curtain on it and an old chair inside. Two holes are cut into the sides of the stall and every girl inducted into the sorority has to sit in that chair and suck off each member of their brother frat, the Omegas." She sat back and raised her eyebrows as I imagined the scene. The girl sitting on the chair in the small aluminum shower stall, her stomach tight with nerves and excitement. Thick, hard cocks sliding through the openings, the tips glistening with precum. The girl would open wide and take the length in her mouth, not knowing which guy she was sucking. And once that man had finished, his cum thick and warm in her mouth, she would turn to take the next one waiting on her other side.

"Earth to Jay," Jessie said with a smug smile. "Come back from the land of jizz."

I rolled my eyes, but my blush betrayed where my thoughts had strayed.

"It is kind of hot, isn't it?" She lit a cigarette as if she had been the one in my fantasy sucking off each frat man. "Gets me a little charged up thinking about it."

I sighed. "Okay, so the Omegas have a shower stall glory hole in their basement. What's that got to do with us?"

A slow, vaguely lewd smile drifted across Jessie's lips. "You like Kevin Sanderson." I nodded and she continued. "Kevin told us when we saw him in the library this week that he was going to be rushing the Omega house tomorrow night." I nodded again. "Old Glory is in the basement of Omega house." I narrowed my eyes but remained silent as she continued. "I think we can set it up for you to be able to suck off your dream man and he wouldn't be any wiser."

I took a breath and tried to ignore the solid column of sex cramped inside my jeans. It was a ridiculous, possibly dangerous, idea. But I was so turned on by the prospect of tasting Kevin Sanderson's cock, I pushed all reason aside and said, "Tell me."

My roommate, Keith, drove home every Friday evening to see his girlfriend on the weekend, and when I awoke in my dorm room on Saturday morning, alone, my cock was up and ready. As I stroked the rigid length of my cock, I imagined Kevin Sanderson as my roommate.

Kevin would awaken suddenly on Saturday morning and catch me masturbating. He would get out of his bed and approach mine, his gaze fastened on the fat, slick head of my dick, his own erection tenting the front of his boxers. Our eyes would meet for a single, heated moment before his face dropped flat into my crotch, his throat devouring the entire hot poker of my cock in one swallow. I would let out a moan and press my hands to the back of his head, fingers curling in the soft waves of his hair, and then I would hump his face. My hips would bounce up off the thin university mattress as my cock rammed down his throat. He would squeeze his beautiful dark eyes shut and his lips would swell from the onslaught of my dick until, finally, with a low groan, I would pump my thick, heavy load into his mouth. He would swallow it down his throat, sucking my cock dry, and then climb onto my bed and straddle my face to jerk himself off, his cock hard and heavy, a regular battering ram. As I sucked on his hairy, sweat-slick balls, I would watch the blur of his hand as it narrowed its focus to a spot, *the* spot, just beneath the purple ridge of his head.

There would be a moment, a bare fraction of a moment, when he was suspended between masturbation and orgasm. His eyes would open and he would smile down at me just before he shot off, his eyes glazed with lustful love and his breath smelling of my cum. And then my face would be covered by his warm, fragrant spunk. I could almost hear the wet *pop* as it blasted with force from the narrow piss slit to land thick and hot on my face and in my mouth. After he coaxed the last of it from his cock, squeezed a final drop from the head to land in my open mouth, he would plop the softening mass of his dick on my tongue and I would suck even more out of him, watching his glowing, sleep-lined face as I nursed contentedly.

I usually came well before I got to the part where I stared up at Kevin straddling my chest, but I knew how the fantasy ended; I ran it through my head during boring lectures or while walking to and from class. Afterward, I lay in bed for a time and surfed the afterglow of my orgasm, the semen drying on my belly until I forced myself to get out of bed and clean up with tissues before trotting down the hall to the community showers.

The night of the Omega party, I dressed in a maroon shirt and jeans, then sat fidgeting in the lobby awaiting Jessie. She breezed in the main doors like a spring wind, her blouse unbuttoned to provide an eyeful of her ample cleavage and her hair styled in red waves. She gave off no hint of nervousness as she linked her arm through mine and led me out into the cool September night. As we walked in silence through the chill darkness, she lit a cigarette and gave me a sidelong look.

"You're nervous."

I brayed a high-pitched laugh. "What? Why? Do I look nervous?"

"Considering you just laughed like a donkey, yeah, I'd say you look nervous. Do you not want to go through with this?"

I swallowed the lump in my throat as the Omega house came into view, every window glowing and the thump of music audible even at this distance. "No, I want to do it. I'm just scared, that's all. There's so much that could go wrong."

"Ah, true," Jessie said and flicked the stub of her filter off into the night. "But there's also so much that can go right."

I nodded and we paused at the foot of the walk leading to the crowded Omega front porch as I took a breath. "Okay," I said, with what I hoped was a firm set to my jaw. "I'm ready."

Jessie assessed me for a moment then nodded and smiled. "I think you are at that. Come on then, here we go."

We squeezed in the front door, paid our cover and, clutching empty cups, headed for the kitchen. The Omega house was large and every vacant spot seemed filled by a person or piece of furniture. We shouldered our way to the keg stuck into a tub of ice by the back door and waited in line, talking with people we both knew from classes and the cafeteria.

When I got up to the keg, I was surprised to find a well-built, bald-headed man with a goatee and no shirt standing behind and supervising the allocation of beer. He gripped a long, raunchy-smelling cigar in his teeth and squinted against the smoke blowing into his face and out the open back door behind him. His chest was hard with muscle, covered with thin dark hair, and I noticed that his nipples had hardened from the breeze coming in the open door behind him. He was very handsome in a masculine way, a man built to fuck and almost bursting with testosterone.

He moved his eyes to take in Jessie's fabulous cleavage and grinned around the soggy end of his cigar. "Well, hello there angel."

Jessie grinned and handed him her cup. "Hello back, you hairy-chested beast."

He laughed heartily as he drew her a beer. "And a beast I am at that." He tipped her a wink and, without taking his eyes from her breasts, reached out for my empty cup and filled it with finesse. A born bartender.

"Come back and see me sometime," he called after us as we turned to make our way through the crowd.

"Okay," Jessie said over her shoulder and smiled before turning her back and rolling her eyes. "Frat boys."

I risked a look back to find the keg man already talking up another girl. "You don't think he's attractive?"

She shook her head. "I like my men a little stronger in the brains department." We stopped in an open spot against a wall and drank our beer as we searched the room.

"I don't see him," I said. "Maybe he went home for the weekend or something?"

"I doubt it," Jessie said. "Give him time, he'll show up."

And moments later, as if summoned by her words, Kevin Sanderson stepped through the front door. He paid his cover and accepted his cup. Moving through the crowd, he nodded and spoke to each person as he made his way to the kitchen, passing us without a second look. Disappointment welled up inside me. How could he have overlooked us? Jessie sensed my plunge in mood and leaned down to whisper in my ear.

"Don't worry, horn dog, he won't overlook us for long."

Her confidence comforted me and I sipped my beer. Moments later, Kevin appeared in the kitchen doorway, arm raised to keep from spilling his beer. He threaded his way through the crowd of people and just as he was about to pass us by, he glanced our way. He did a slight double take at the sight of Jessie then seemed to notice me standing beside her. His hips turned and he smiled as he approached.

"Hey, you two," he said. "You decided to rush Omega, too, Jay?"

"He's considering his options," Jessie said, sounding like my agent or lawyer. She flashed him a bright smile and I watched with a touch of jealousy as Kevin's eyes took a dive into her bosom.

"Yes, well, I can see you've dressed for the occasion," he said and turned to me. "How'd your history test go this week?"

I stood in stunned silence for a moment, amazed that Kevin remembered a brief discussion we had had in passing on campus. Jessie elbowed me lightly and I blinked and stuttered a response. "I—I...it went okay. I guess. Never can tell with history. If it's not one war it's another, you know?"

Kevin smiled and nodded. "I know just what you mean."

Jessie stepped in and began talking with him, flirting openly as she laughed at everything he said and tossed her hair and reached out to touch his arm every so often. I stood to the side and watched all this with a sinking heart, wondering if maybe this wasn't such a good idea after all. What if Kevin and Jessie started going out? How would I feel about that?

I excused myself to get a refill on my beer and pushed my way into the kitchen. The cigar-smoking keg keeper was talking with a group of tall, athletic men when I approached and he squinted down at me as he idly scratched his thick, blunt

fingers over his bare chest. I wet my lips and looked up at his
rugged face with what I hoped was a neutral expression.

"Yeah?" he said around the stub of his cigar.

"May I have a refill, please?"

He grinned. "You're a polite one." He considered me a
moment then nodded. "All right, but only because you said
please."

I tried not to let my eyes roam his body as he refilled my cup,
but couldn't help noticing his nipples were still hard brown
nubs beneath the fine dark hair. I dropped my gaze altogether
when he handed my cup back and I turned to go.

"Hey!" he called and I gave a little jump and turned to look
back at him. "You forgot to say thank you."

"Oh, sorry. Thanks."

"You're welcome." He gave me a grin to let me know he was
really no threat, and I turned away, breathing a sigh of relief as
I made my way out of the kitchen. Once I passed through to the
dining room, I stopped and stared at the spot where I had left
Kevin and Jessie talking. They were nowhere in sight.

In a slight panic, I turned to search out the door to the basement and realized with a sinking gut that it stood behind the
keeper of the keg. He was guarding the way to the basement,
the place I needed to be waiting for Jessie and Kevin.

I tried to decide what to do when I noticed the back door
standing open behind the handsome, bare-chested keg keeper.
There was some room behind him for me to creep past and
down the steps into the basement. I would need to be quiet, but
it was possible.

Fighting off a sinking feeling of doom, I chugged my beer
and headed out the front door, trying to act as inconspicuous
as possible as I circled to the back yard. I stood in the shadows
outside the back door for a moment, gathering my resolve.

Off in the bushes I heard the breathy exclamations of a couple making out and wondered, briefly, if it was Jessie and Kevin. I decided it was best for me not to know how Jessie planned to lure Kevin into the basement for me, just to be thankful that she was doing this at all.

I squared my shoulders and headed for the steps leading to the open back door just as the broad shoulders of the keg keeper filled the doorframe. His head was turned as he talked to someone in the kitchen so he could not see me standing just a few feet away. He took another drag on his cigar then tossed it out into the yard before turning back to his duties at the keg. I ducked beneath the glowing missile and listened to the hiss of the burning end die as it hit the wet grass behind me.

With my nerves screaming, I eased up the creaking wooden steps and stood just outside the door. The back of the keg keeper's shaved head gleamed in the reflection of the glass in the back door, and I waited for the perfect moment when his attention was diverted. When I saw my chance, I stepped quickly, quietly into the house and started down the basement steps. Three steps down I paused, waiting for someone to call out for me to stop, but no voices followed me and I made my way into the cool, damp basement.

One bare bulb illuminated the cavernous room and I carefully wound my way around piles of rank laundry, a dozen mud-splattered mountain bikes, a set of old, rusted patio furniture, and boxes marked CHRISTMAS DECORATIONS. As I explored the bowels of the Omega house, I took in the underwear and T-shirts scattered around the floor in the general area of the washer and dryer and wondered if the keg keeper's underwear was part of this group.

A footstep on the stairs and a girl's giggle made me jump and I ducked behind the steps, emerging on the other side of the basement where I found Old Glory. It stood in shadow in the middle of that section of the basement and was just as Jessie had described it: an old aluminum shower stall with a dark curtain hanging open in the doorway. Inside the stall waited an old, padded vinyl kitchen chair.

Another step on the stairs followed by a deep huff of laughter goaded me into action and I entered the small enclosure and sat on the chair. I pulled the curtain closed, shutting out the feeble light from across the room as I tried not to hyperventilate. My stomach was knotted but my cock was hard and pulsed painfully against its denim prison.

I took in the holes cut into either side of the stall. Stains ran down the wall from each of the holes, and I considered the great number of horny, hung fraternity men who had shot their wads with their cocks poking into this room. I licked my lips then grew still and listened as the girl giggled again, closer this time. Moving from the seat, I crouched in a corner behind the chair and waited.

A deep voice murmured persuasively and I held my breath. This was it; this was what I had been dreaming of for months now. I was going to suck Kevin Sanderson off.

The curtain slid aside and I watched a shadowy form stumble giggling into the stall. A strong, masculine hand guided her to the chair and I tried to catch a glimpse of Kevin's face, but Jessie's silhouette blocked my view. The smell of cigarette smoke and beer assured me this was, indeed, Jessie sitting before me.

"Just stay right there," the man said, his voice deepened with lust. "Okay?"

"Uh-huh," the girl moaned, her head drooping.

The curtain dropped closed and I listened to the man step around to the left of the stall, the wall I crouched against. The figure before me slumped over and slid off the chair and I got

up to take her place. I had just leaned down to make sure Jessie
was okay when I heard the steady sound of a zipper being
opened.

"Open your mouth and close your eyes," Kevin said, "it's
time for a big surprise."

A long, thick cock slid through the hole by my face. It gave
off a pale glow in the dim light from the single bulb across the
basement, but from what I could see of it, it was a beauty. It
was wide and tall, capped by a meaty head slick with glistening
precum.

Instinctively, I opened wide, glad I had remembered to shave
closely before I got dressed for the party, and took the solid
length deep in my throat. On the other side of the wall I heard
Kevin let out a deep groan, followed by a whispered, "Oh,
fuck."

The rigid column of flesh in my mouth pulsed with heat and
I slowly dragged my lips up to the tip. It was thicker than I had
estimated, and I pursed my lips around the silken head, sucking
with increasing pressure as Kevin sighed and moaned on the
other side of the wall.

"Oh, yeah," he said quietly. "Suck on the head like that.
Now take it all, baby, deep throat it for me."

I obliged, closing my eyes as I leaned forward and pressed
my lips into the bush of his pubic hair. I inhaled his sweaty,
manly scent and eased my lips back to the bulbous head where
I sucked harder. Through the wall I heard whispered curses
of encouragement, things like, "Fuck, yeah," and "Suck that
fuckin' log," and I longed to free my own cock and jerk off in
time, but was self-conscious of Jessie lying on the floor behind
me. Instead, I pressed my hand against the hard lump of erection
in my jeans and fought against the urge to moan in response.

I imagined how his cock would feel in my ass, could see

myself standing up and dropping my pants, turning my ass up to receive him. I longed to feel the blunt, slick tip push past my sphincter and burrow into my body; feel it scrape against my prostate and push my cum up from my nuts. At the thought of Kevin inside me, filling me, I huffed out a quiet breath and sucked him even harder.

"Oh, god, you really know how to suck cock," he groaned. "I just want to fuck your mouth."

He thrust his hips, his cock plunging into my throat and pulling out faster and faster, and I held my head still to allow him to pump between my lips. Through the stall, I heard him grunt, an animal sound that came from deep in his chest, and a moment later I received his rush of semen. I swallowed the thick, ropy stuff, savoring the taste, and he gasped with each shot.

I sucked him a little longer then let the long, fat dick drop from my mouth. I wiped my mouth with my forearm and turned to Jessie's still form, the smell of beer, cigarette smoke, and cum mingling in the hot, still air of the small room.

"Oh, god," Kevin whispered, his cock hanging through the hole in the wall as he caught his breath. "Oh, fuck, that was hot."

I shook Jessie to let her know I was finished and felt a flicker of panic when she did not stir. Her breathing was heavy as though she had passed out, but Jessie had not had a lot to drink. I reached out to part the curtain slightly and allowed a feeble touch of light to illuminate the girl's face. It was not Jessie. It was no one I recognized, and I realized suddenly that I had not sucked off Kevin Sanderson, but some unknown man who, in moments, would be zipping his pants and walking around to open the curtain, expecting to find he had been blown by his girlfriend and not some freshman boy.

Turning, I watched the stranger's cock slowly withdraw, and then I slipped out through the curtain, making my way around to the back of Old Glory as the man stepped to the front. He parted the curtain and asked, "Hey, babe, you okay?"

I listened as he tried to wake her up, but, when she proved to be unresponsive, he grumbled something about "fuckin' chicks who can't hold their beer," and hefted her over his shoulder. As he stomped off across the basement, I peered around the corner of Old Glory and caught sight of him as he passed beneath the bare lightbulb across the room. It was the keg keeper, his shirt still off and his back muscles working as he moved to the steps with the unconscious girl slung over his shoulder.

I sat with my back against the wall of Old Glory and caught my breath, the taste of the keg keeper's cum thick in my throat as I went through my options. I could stay in the basement and wait to see if Jessie was able to convince Kevin to let her blow him, or creep up the basement steps and steal outside to rejoin the party and look for Jessie.

The cold of the concrete floor bit into my ass and I decided it was time to vacate the basement. God only knew how many other Omegas were going to come down to get blown. I sighed and got to my feet, my legs stiff from the cold floor, then made my way to the steps and snuck back up to the main level. I waited until I heard the keg keeper's voice as he returned to his post, muttering under his breath about the chick passed out in his bedroom, then I stepped quickly out the back door. I stole through the dark yard to the front where I found Jessie and Kevin standing on the sidewalk in front of the house. Jessie's eyes widened at the sight of me and she exhaled a thick plume of smoke as Kevin turned and smiled.

"Hey," Kevin said as I approached them. "We were wondering where you got off to."

"Ah, um," I stammered and blushed, finding I could not look at either of them. "I went to get a beer and then stood in line for the bathroom and just lost track of you two, I guess." I glanced quickly at Jessie to find her giving me a studious look.

"Yeah, those bathroom lines can stretch on for hours," Kevin said. "We thought you got lost or something. We were starting to worry."

Jessie nodded to me. "Kevin was very concerned about you. Kept asking where you had got off to." She winked and I felt my heavy heart suddenly buoy in my chest.

"Well, yeah," Kevin looked back to the house, embarrassed. "I just hoped nothing had happened to you, that's all. You never know what can happen at these parties with all this beer." He shrugged and I almost sighed at the boyishness of the action.

"Okay then," Jessie said and flicked her cigarette into the street. "I guess it's time Jay and I headed home. His roommate's gone for the weekend and I bet he's got something special lined up."

My eyes grew round as I stared at her and then I turned back to Kevin. "Uh, not really. Just laundry."

"Well, maybe I can come by tomorrow and we can hang out or something," Kevin said.

The words *or something* echoed in my head and I nodded, a stupid smile on my face. "Yeah. Sure. That would be great."

I recited my cell phone number and he tapped it into his phone. He gave Jessie a clumsy hug before he turned to me. "I'll call you tomorrow."

"Good. Okay. Great." I closed my eyes a moment and held my tongue, then looked at Jessie for help but she was grinning at me, apparently enjoying watching me dig myself in deeper. I turned back to Kevin. "Sorry. Too much beer, I guess. So, call me. Tomorrow. And we can get together."

Kevin grinned and, in the glow of a nearby streetlight, I thought I caught a glimpse of depravity in his eyes that made my cock jerk. "Sounds good."

Jessie and I walked off down the sidewalk, side stepping around some drunks staggering toward us, and she linked her arm through mine.

"He wouldn't go down there with me," she said, her eyes fixed straight ahead. "I offered and he very politely turned me down."

"Oh, I see." I couldn't think of anything else to say and was unsure whether I wanted to tell her I had ended up sucking off the cigar-smoking keg keeper.

"Did you go down there?" she asked, still not looking at me.

My mind was racing. How much should I tell her? "Well, yeah, I was down there waiting but you never showed up."

"What was down there?" she asked, finally turning to me. "Is it like they say?"

I nodded. "Exactly. An old shower stall, holes cut into the sides with a curtain in front."

She smiled and her eyes glittered like jewels in the halcyon light. "I knew it. Those sluts." She looked back at me and, still smiling, said, "You too."

"What?" I tried to look innocent.

She leaned in close and sniffed at my breath. "You need to brush your teeth before you talk to anyone else."

I groaned and slapped my palm against my head.

"Who was it?" she asked.

"You wouldn't believe me if I told you."

"Try me," she said.

I told her the story and her high, ringing laughter lifted my spirits. Maybe this night hadn't been a total fuck-up after all.

"You can't tell," I said. "No one. Ever."

"Not even the keg keeper?" she asked with a teasing grin.

"Especially him!" I nearly shrieked. "He'd kill me."

"Yeah, club you to death with that big cock of his."

We laughed together at that, but I made her cross her heart and promise never to tell another living soul. With that settled, we set a course for my dorm as I wondered what Kevin and I would find to do the next day.

NEW LAMBDA

Kyle Lukoff

Before you get any ideas about my frat, let me set you straight. We are first and foremost a social brotherhood, dedicated to enriching the lives of the young men who choose to pledge. There are no traumatic hazing rituals, no forced keg-stands or gerbil shenanigans. Instead, anyone who wants to join our fraternity has to complete a pledge project that shows his commitment to the community at large. Each pledge is assigned a big brother who helps him through the pledge process, in the spirit of fostering unity and connection.

Our fraternity, Nu Lambda, may be the nation's oldest fraternity for men of diverse sexual orientations, but it is not, I repeat *not*, some sort of porn director's wet dream. We have a strict code of ethics that each brother promises to uphold during his time here. We are not a dating or hookup club; that's what the Gay Student Union is for. We sponsor buses to Washington, DC for the Marriage Equality March and write letters to our congressmen about local and federal nondiscriminatory employment policies. We believe that we have a duty to promote a positive image of what the modern gay man looks like. Needless to say, none of us are drag queens.

My name is Nicholas Ashworth III, and I am a senior here at Lincoln University. I knew I wanted to rush NL as soon as I saw their table during the activities fair during new student orientation. I had come out as gay during high school, but never felt like I fit in with the rest of the kids at the gay youth group I went to once a month. Some of them were street kids, a couple were goths, most of them had at least one visible piercing or tattoo. I made friends with a lesbian who was the valedictorian at a nearby high school, but other than that I didn't really socialize with them outside of group.

I had, of course, done my research about which fraternity I wanted to join and had pretty much settled on Kappa Delta Chi. I knew that Lincoln U had a gay frat, but I had planned to stay away. Being homosexual was just one part of my identity, not something I thought I had to focus on. But on my way past the different student groups I noticed a table with a tasteful red-and-white flag and a gorgeous young man standing behind it. He flashed me a toothy smile, and I stopped by his table without thinking twice.

"Hi there," he said, "My name's Ethan. Have you heard about Nu Lambda?"

"Uh, no. I mean, yes, but I didn't think… No. No, I haven't." I blushed, hearing how stupid I sounded.

"Well, let me tell you a little about us." He gave me a little speech about brotherhood and community and accountability, which I barely listened to, and in a daze I agreed to go to the first informational meeting.

I know what you're thinking. I go to this meeting, meet Ethan formally, endure some hot hazing initiation and we have a lot of sex. But that's not how it went at all. Instead of some hot one-night stand I found an entire network of friends and brothers. At one point during sophomore year I had a boyfriend, but to be honest my fraternity responsibilities, along with my course load and the work I did with the campus Democrats didn't leave me much time to date. I knew it was the same with the other guys in the frat. We were all busy with some organization or another, a lot of us were premed or prelaw, and we were all committed to furthering gay rights.

One day toward the end of my senior year I was hanging out on the quad with my best friend, Kristy. We had met during freshman orientation—I complimented her on her strappy red heels, and she immediately adopted me as fag to her hag.

Today, like most days, we were complaining about men.

"You just don't get it, Nick. It's way harder to be straight than to be gay. Nowadays there's, like, the Gay Democrats, and the Out Laws, and the Gay Student Union. It's gotta be so easy to find boys to hook up with. It's not like there's some sort of Straight Student's Union or something where I can meet boys, I just gotta try my luck with the general population. There's no way to really sort out the assholes from the good guys."

"No, Kristy, you're the one who doesn't get it. All the guys in the Gay Democrats already have partners, and if they don't, there's a good reason why. And the Gay Student Union? Puh-lease! All they care about are, like, prostitutes and transsexuals and homeless teenagers. People that are nothing like me. Besides, have you seen those guys? They all wear ripped hoodies with ANARCHY patches on them. I sure wouldn't want to bring a boy like that home to Mother."

Kristy sighed. "Damn. And here I was thinking that all I had to do was turn lez, and everything would suddenly be so much easier."

"No way. All the lesbians on this campus wear Birkenstocks and don't shave their legs."

"Ew! That's so gross!" With that she flopped down onto the grass, putting her hand dramatically on her forehead.

I tried to pull her up. "Honey, you'll get grass stains on your skirt!"

"I don't care! No one's ever going to love me!"

"Don't be silly. You're so sexy; I bet all those straight guys in the other fraternities would just die to get inside your cute little panties."

She pouted. "You think so?"

"Honey, I know so. Look, how's this?" I got up and crossed over to a pillar thickly plastered with fliers advertising different campus events. I ripped off one for the annual Delta Gamma Theta Spring Fling and took it back over to where she was sprawled out on the grass again.

I brandished the flier in front of her face. "The Spring Fling. I bet you one hundred dollars that you get laid as a result of this party."

"A hundred bucks?"

"Yeah. If no one asks you out on a date, I'll give you one hundred dollars. If someone does, then you name your first child after me."

"What if I go to the party and, like, wear a pair of big ugly glasses or don't comb my hair?"

"I know you too well, girl. You want to get married by the time you're twenty-five, and college is almost over! There's no way you'd go to this party and not try to find a date."

She smacked me on the arm, but giggled. "You're right. And it's been so long since I hooked up with someone...not since Trent during spring break, remember?"

"I remember. I practically had to pry the Ben and Jerry's out of your hands when he stopped calling."

"Okay, it's a bet. You'll go with me though, right?"

I stopped short. "With you? To a straight frat-boy party? I don't know. Those boys make me nervous."

"Nervous? How come? They're mostly sweethearts."

"To you, maybe. Not to a fag like me. And besides, they're all so hot. I'd probably get a boner or something, and end up the poster boy for hate crime legislation."

"But I can't go without you! What if I end up date-raped or something?"

"That doesn't really happen, right?"

"I mean, I don't know, but just in case. Please go with me?"

I thought about it. I had been to some of the parties at the straight frat houses, but they had always been fancy networking events with alumni or members of the administration. Other brothers I knew had gone to some of the regular kegger parties, but they were all more straight-acting than me. Not that I was a limp-wristed queen or anything, but I liked my Dockers perfectly pressed, and when I got drunk my lisp would come out.

But maybe I could just go as Kristy's wingman. That way I could stick near her for safety. And while I truly did want her to get a date, I also didn't want her to be happily coupled while I was still single. By staying near her I could scare off some of her potential suitors.

"Okay," I said, "I'll go with you. So long as you promise not to abandon me as soon as some hottie turns his baby blues on you."

"Only if you promise the same."

I laughed. "At the DGT party? Not gonna happen. But it's a deal."

Plans made, we went out for happy hour and spent the rest of the night talking about what Kristy was going to wear. Toward the end of the night she began chatting with a football player, and I tactfully made my way home.

The night of the party quickly approached. I got together my butchest outfit, a pair of Levi's and a black shirt with matching Converse.

I met Kristy at the campus gates. "You look smashing!" She was wearing a little black dress and pumps with a wrought-silver necklace and earrings.

"Thanks, cutie." She kissed me on the cheek and tucked her arm into the crook of my arm. We walked over to the DGT house together, easily distinguishable from all the other stately houses on the block, since it was lit up from roof to basement and throbbing with hip-hop music. I took a deep breath, steeled myself and walked in with Kristy.

Oh. My. My jaw dropped, but I closed my mouth quickly before anyone noticed. It was like walking into a porno shoot. Hot men were all around, a veritable buffet of boys. Blond, brunet, redhead. Pale, tanned, freckled. All were tall and muscular—Delta Theta Gamma was for "men demonstrating academic and athletic excellence," so they were buff as hell and pulled at least a B average. Kristy nudged me with her elbow. "Not bad, right?" she whispered.

"Not bad at all."

With that we headed over to the bar and got drinks. We found a bare expanse of wall and stationed ourselves against it, sipping our drinks. Boys eddied around us, talking, laughing, casting occasional glances in Kristy and my direction. For a while we just stared, but soon the alcohol started to have an effect and we started chatting with each other. Kristy giggled every time one of the boys looked at her, and I tried to gaze nonchalantly into the middle distance.

I couldn't have been bored if I tried, staring at all that gorgeous, unattainable male flesh, but Kristy started to get a little antsy.

"Can we wander around a little?" she asked. "I want to see the rest of the house.

"Sure." I was starting to feel a little self-conscious, just standing against the wall like that. We walked around the house, and on the second floor Kristy ran into some friends from her sorority, a few of them already in conversation with some guys. I stood off to the side while the girls giggled and flirted and just looked around the room.

Suddenly the most beautiful example of manhood I had ever seen waltzed into my line of sight. He was tall and blond with a sprinkling of freckles atop his Grecian nose and sea-green eyes. I gulped and managed a tremulous smile when he looked my way. He narrowed his eyes and looked me up and down. Appraisal complete, he broke out into a toothy grin and came toward me.

"Hi," he said in a deep voice, "I'm Ryan."

"Uh, Nicky. Um, Nicholas. I mean, Nick. I'm Nick."

Suddenly the girls' attention all turned to us.

"Ryan, did you say?" asked one of Kristy's friends.

"Hi, Ryan!" said Kristy, grabbing his hand to shake it.

"Ryan! Remember me? We had freshman English together!" said another. I was pushed aside as Ryan was overwhelmed by a sea of purses and feathered hair and desperation.

I sighed and backed away. No doubt Kristy would spend the rest of her night vying for Ryan's affections. I ascended the flight of stairs behind us, looking for the bathroom, and gloomily I imagined myself to be out a C-note.

Halfway up the staircase a hand clapped onto my shoulder.

"Hey, Nick, so how about that meeting?"

I turned. There was Ryan on the step behind me, with a very disappointed gaggle of girls pouting in our direction.

"Meeting? Huh?"

"You're Nick Ashworth from Nu Lambda, right? I told the ladies you and I had to talk about interfraternity relations with a few of my brothers. Come on, let's go upstairs."

I was a little confused, but I followed Ryan up the stairs, down the hallway, through a door he unlocked with a key hidden behind a poster, and into...

"Oh. Man. What the..." I was president of the Philologist Society and still found myself at a loss for words.

"This is why you came, right? You NL boys never come to any of our parties; maybe you'll tell your bros what they've been missing."

The room was darkened. A flat-screen TV against the far wall was casting a flickering light. I glanced at it, and my eyes were greeted with a bare ass, low-hanging balls and a huge dick pounding into what could only be another man's ass. Afraid to be caught looking at gay porn I looked away, but it was like the image on the screen was replicated a dozen times over. Boys were everywhere, boxers or tighty-whities down around their ankles or flung across the room, sports jerseys and muscle tees and Lincoln U shirts strewn all around.

"What...what's going on? I thought...is this...I mean, aren't you all...?"

"Aren't we all what?"

"Uh, I mean, I'm in the, you know, that other frat, for, um, guys who...um, GLB...I mean, G...I mean, you know what I mean!"

"You mean aren't we all straight?"

"Well, uh, yeah."

Ryan shook his head. "Nicky, Nicky, Nicky. You boys in Nu

Lambda have a lot to learn." With that he shoved me into the fray.

I couldn't tell you what all happened to me that night if I tried. I remember taking part in a circle jerk, with one man's hard tool in my right hand and mine being pumped by another, all of us grunting and straining, busting out with loud orgasms one after another, thick white cum splattering on us like a rainstorm.

I also remember being on my hands and knees, my tongue exploring the underside of someone's sweaty balls until he grabbed me by the hair and shoved his cock deep down my throat. Tears streamed down my face as I struggled to take his whole shaft, and when I finally found a rhythm, another brother got behind me and slowly worked first his fingers, then his meat into my ass. When the first boy's load streamed down my throat he pulled out of my mouth and lay down beneath me to reciprocate. My speaking abilities long gone, I was reduced to a moaning mess, wordless exultation coming out of my mouth as I rammed myself back and forth between competing pleasures.

Oh, it was a long night. Apparently fisting didn't go out of style in the eighties. I found this out when I was forearm-deep in one of our wide receivers. I also learned that Spin the Bottom is a lot more fun than Spin the Bottle. I even drank my first Racehorse—look it up if you don't know what that is.

Before I knew it, the sky outside the one window turned a light shade of gray, and one by one the boys slipped out the door. I looked around the room and gathered up my clothes, all of them rank and sticky. Before I could get dressed Ryan came up from behind and put his arm around my shoulder.

"Hey, why don't you take a shower?" He gestured toward the bathroom. I stumbled in and stood for a good long time under the hot water, watching all evidence of last night's debauchery flow down the drain. When I finally came out there was a clean towel neatly folded on the toilet seat lid and underneath that a pair of jeans and a university T-shirt in just my size. I put them on and stepped out into the room, now lit by the rising sun.

Ryan had straightened things up while I was showering, and as I watched he threw the rest of the dripping condoms into a big black garbage bag.

When he saw me he stretched his arms over his head and yawned. "Come on, let's go get some breakfast. I'll explain after I've had some coffee."

Still speechless I followed him to the twenty-four-hour diner just down University Way. True to his word, after he'd drunk the first cup of coffee and our eggs and toast were ordered, he began to talk.

"All the other guys know that they can have a good time at our place. I'm gay, and a few of the other guys in that room would also say so, but most of us just want to, you know, come and go as we please. To hear the straight dudes tell it, all the girls on this campus just want to get married—you can only fuck them if you tell them that you love them. There's none of that with us, it's all just for fun."

"How come I never heard of this before?" I was dumb-founded. There were secret gay orgies happening just a few doors down from my house, and no one ever told me?

"Some of your brothers know about it. One or two might come, rarely, but in general they disapprove. I once heard a Lambda boy say that we 'give gay men a bad name.' Funny, I never wanted a good name in the first place."

"So you're all just closet cases? Is that why I've never seen any of you at the Marriage Equality or Don't Ask, Don't Tell protests?"

Ryan glared at me. "I am *not* closeted. I just don't care about getting married or joining the fucking army. That shit's for straight people. What I don't get is why guys like you feel the need to turn us into happy homemakers and soldiers. What you saw last night? *That* is what being gay is about. While you're planning what kind of rice you want thrown on you at your expensive fruity wedding, I'll be having sex."

He paused his lecture as the waiter set down our plates of breakfast, and I took the opportunity to jump in.

"But what about equality?"

He shoveled a forkful of egg in his mouth before responding. "Dude, look in the mirror. You're white. You're a man. And aren't you, like, Nicholas Ashworth THE THIRD? I don't think you need to worry too much about equality."

Now it was my turn to glare. "Gay people are still second-class citizens."

"*Some* gay people are. You, my friend, are not. End of story."

That didn't seem like the end of the story to me, but I shut up and ate my breakfast. We finished up, split the bill and headed out.

Ryan didn't change my mind about anything immediately. But the next week I stopped by a meeting of the Queer Student Union, to see what those kids thought was important. And the next year I skipped a big marriage equality rally for one of their parties.

FRAT CONTEST
GONE WILD

Jay Starre

The scene was set. The first contestant shed his clothes in a rush; his dark eyes fixed on the huge, hot ass perched on the cushioned bench in front of him.

The Louisiana night was warm and humid. The rooftop of the frat chapter house was open to the moonlight on one side and overhung by oaks dripping Spanish moss on the remaining sides. A trio of floodlights illuminated the masked jock that would be the focus of the student film about to take place.

Christoph stood beside Gabriel in the shadows. He grinned triumphantly as he watched his nemesis, Beau, the star tackle on their college football team, look back apprehensively at the approaching student about to dive into his beautiful, big butt.

Revenge was a dish best served cold, he'd heard. It had been a year now since he'd pledged Theta Gamma Phi. Pledge week had been hell, mostly due to Beau, who'd seemed to derive great pleasure from humiliating him in as many ways as possible. The giant football tackle had relished doling out the most demeaning of the pledge tasks to Christoph in particular. Cleaning the toilets naked, on all fours, while being paddled being one of the worst. None of it had been really brutal, but Christoph was a proud person and hadn't taken the humiliation well.

That pride stemmed from his background. His family was Creole, the mixed-race Louisiana locals who had been a breed unto themselves during the years of slavery, often considering themselves better than both blacks and whites. Some people claimed he was stuck-up, and they weren't entirely off the mark.

So his anger at Beau had festered until just this past week, when he'd come up with the plot that had the massive tackle on *his* hands and knees, gigantic ass in the air, awaiting the initial contestant who was about to do his best to win the first ever Theta Gamma Phi "ass-eating challenge!"

Kevin Chow was that first frat brother up. Each contestant was allowed to place the star football player in one position, and the Korean-American was going for a meal from behind. His dark eyes gleamed in the glow of the floodlights Gabriel had managed to score from the art department. His smooth and lanky brown body twitched as he moved in to clutch those gigantic jock mounds and spread them.

He buried his cute, brown face between the milky-pale cheeks and began to munch.

Christoph was in charge of music and he immediately switched off the dramatic trumpet and clarinet medley he'd opened with. Now, only the music of the Louisiana night, the sounds of croaking frogs and cicadas, created a backdrop for the nasty slurps and smacks of their first contestant as he sought to eat out football ass as best he could.

Christoph had sprung wood the moment Beau shed his clothes and now that throbbing boner pressed against the cotton of his track pants. Beside him, Gabriel played cameraman, a nasty grin on his wide face as he moved in closer.

The tall art student was supposedly brilliant, and Christoph had been careful not to manipulate him into agreeing to this contest too blatantly. He'd approached the subject a week earlier.

"That fraternity short film contest is coming up again. I've got a great idea for it. You know how it always has to be about a contest or a challenge? Well, instead of a pie-eating contest, why don't we set up an ass-eating contest and film that?"

Gabriel's blue eyes sparkled mischievously as he whooped with laughter. "Fuck! Sounds hilarious. That'll really get the judges all hot and bothered. But you know it's more original than all the gross crap we heard got submitted last year, including our own lame one, that burping and farting contest. But who could we get to offer up his butt for an ass-eating contest?"

"There's really only one choice." The success of his revenge plot all hinged on that one and only choice.

The chapter house president thought that over for a few scary heartbeats while Christoph tried to look as innocent as possible. "Of course. You mean Beau. A humongous ass like his would be perfect. And he'd be pretty easy to convince."

That was a nice way of putting it. He wasn't the sharpest tool in the box, and if he hadn't been such an outstanding football player, he'd most likely have been applying for the janitorial position at their college instead of attending it.

Right now, a week later, he didn't look particularly scholastic. He emitted a series of brainless groans as Korean-American tongue drilled into his jock hole from behind. Kevin's brown face rooted deep between those massive mounds while his brown hands clutched at the flushed cheeks, as he attempted to spread them wider and get his tongue deeper into that hot slot.

Gabriel's attempts at getting some good hole shots were

blocked by Kevin's face and body. The only way you could tell what was happening to that asshole was by the loud smacks he made—and the satisfying groans from Beau.

The challenge was set up on a point basis. Contestants scored for enthusiasm, creativity and reaction from their masked star, "Big-Ass Jock," as they'd named Beau for the credits. Kevin was definitely racking up points on the enthusiasm scale and starting to garner more for reaction.

Beau began grunting the moment Kevin's face was shoved into his ass. He arched his back and wriggled that giant butt. Christoph bit his lip and clutched at his stiff cock tenting his sweats as he imagined what was going on. Kevin's tongue must be stabbing far up the jock's twitching pink slot for Beau to be grinding back against his face like that.

Then Kevin blew it, literally. Down between his slim brown thighs, his cock lurched and drooled while he ate jock hole with ravenous focus. All of a sudden, that slender pole swelled up dark purple and without so much as being touched, erupted a geyser of cum.

Gabriel caught it all on camera. Kevin's face was planted deep in Beau's crack as he continued to slurp while his cock spewed out the last of its creamy load.

"Wild, Kevin! Munching on ass while you shoot a big load all over the carpet. Good job, now get the hell out of here. You're done."

There was a time limit for each contestant, which Kevin hadn't exceeded, but there was also a "blow limit": once you blew your nut, your turn was over.

Kevin rose up on shaky legs and grinned a little sheepishly for the camera as he headed for the stairs. He left behind their floodlit star, whose creamy butt boasted two handprints flaming on either hefty cheek.

You couldn't quite see the hole, which was a disappointment for Christoph. Those giant cheeks had a very deep valley between them and even though the giant jock had his knees spread wide, they weren't quite wide enough apart. There was lots of spit on the crack, which Gabriel did his best to get on film.

Beau craned his head around and stared at the pair in charge. His soft blue eyes looked even softer behind his dark mask. That mask was simple and cheap. Bow-shaped, it tied with a string behind his head and obscured part of his forehead, his button-nose and his upper cheeks. His mop of rust-red hair was visible, as were his full pink lips and bold dimpled chin.

He wasn't smiling, but his eyes really shone. He hadn't expected to like it so much, Christoph figured.

It had been even easier than he'd hoped to convince the jock to take on the role of "Big-Ass Jock."

"If we win, it's a thousand bucks for the frat house. That's a lot of stupid car washes we won't have to bother with," Gabriel had promised in his most soothing voice.

"But I don't want any of the guys on the team seeing me getting my butt licked! They know I'm gay, but still I don't want them to see me with my ass in the air and all. It's private stuff," Beau had protested.

Christoph thought it was interesting the giant jock had said he didn't want anyone to see him getting rimmed, but hadn't actually said he didn't want to get his ass eaten.

"Don't worry. We'll give you a mask," he spoke up. It was just the three of them in the chapter house office.

"And no one is going to see the video. It's just the judges who watch them, remember? No one got to see the submissions from last year," Gabriel added.

We'll see about that, Christoph thought, but he maintained a straight face as he spoke. "Besides, it will be a hoot. All those groveling frat brothers with their faces in your ass—you'll come out on top, don't you think?"

"Well, okay, if ya'll think it's a good idea. But I don't want anyone sticking their dick up my butt! Not on camera. Ya'll gotta promise me that."

Gabriel and Christoph agreed immediately, although Christoph kept his true plans to himself.

Now here they were in the steamy Louisiana night with their second contestant stripping and eagerly approaching. Three more were lined up downstairs.

It hadn't been that difficult to rustle up enough challengers from among their frat brothers. After all, most of them were gay or at least bi, and that was no secret. Their fraternity was smirkingly called Theta Gayma Phi by just about everyone at the college.

Also, the object of the ass-eating challenge itself couldn't have been more enticing. The lumbering six foot four, three-hundred-pound tackle was a cum-dream of muscle, and good-looking. Not really arrogant (probably less so than Christoph) he was still considered aloof—mostly because he was so involved with football and nothing else seemed to matter. The opportunity to spread him open and eat him out was a rare treat.

Dean was their resident bodybuilder brother. He spent every free moment in the weight room. With buzzed brown hair and two bright dragon tattoos on each bulging shoulder, he was solid muscle. Yet he was still dwarfed by all that football meat when he knelt between Beau's monster thighs.

"On your back, Brother. Legs in the air and grab your feet."

The gigantic tackle complied, rolling over with a grunt and sprawling back on the bench so that his enormous ass faced the kneeling bodybuilder. He grabbed his own toes and pulled his feet toward his chest.

Dean was smart. He turned and winked at the camera as Gabriel aimed it at the exposed crack. Then he placed his fingers on either side of the jock's puckered pink hole and spread it open.

Christoph found himself trembling. His first sight of that aperture had him breathless. It was shiny with Kevin's spit, and flushed pink against the ivory-white flesh surrounding it. But it was surprisingly snug, considering how eagerly Kevin had drilled it with his tongue.

Dean went to work. He'd obviously thought about it beforehand, probably jerking off while he did, and now he took his time to play it up for the camera. First, he moved in and swiped at the clamping hole with his tongue, the big appendage sticking way out and lapping slowly across the quivering rim.

He managed to keep his face mostly to the side so that Gabriel had a good shot of that hole as it grew more flushed and wet and finally began to quiver open. It was expert work.

As far as reaction went, Dean had chosen a great position for their star. His cock was bared, and although it had been lying semisoft on his belly when it all started, it quickly grew fatter and stiffer as that wide tongue lapped and tickled the exposed butt-lips.

What you could see of Beau's face around the mask was in perfect view too. His soft, blue eyes gleamed behind fluttering eyelids as he half closed them. His mouth, small in a broad chubby face, boasted pink lips that gaped open like a fish out of water as he breathed in and out heavily. His dimpled chin quivered.

His massive thighs, pulled back and spread wide, began to jerk as Dean pointed the tip of his tongue and began to delve beyond the puckered lips of his convulsing asshole.

Big points so far!

Dean did an excellent job of swiping that pouting hole with his fat tongue, tickling it and even thrusting beyond the slowly swelling lips. He ran his tongue up and down the length of Beau's smooth crack, teasing the perineum and even lapping just under the dangling balls.

Christoph found it very interesting, and very hot, that Beau apparently shaved his balls. The fat pair dangled down from the base of his thick cock smooth and pink. He was mostly hairless, with a smattering of reddish hair on his chest between his giant pecs, a little on his forearms and a discernable down on his legs, but in his crotch, his scant bush of red was clearly cut in a straight line just above his 'nads and smooth below.

The notion of the big football jock taking the time to shave those fat balls was such a turn-on Christoph could hardly stand it. He struggled to keep his cool, as his plotted revenge was still far from consummated.

Dean did not keep his cool. Settling over that distended, spit-dripping jock hole, he began to suck loudly, moaning deep in his throat. He reached down and grabbed at his cock. A few rapid pumps of the fat pipe rearing between his naked thighs, and he went out in a blaze of spewing glory.

"Well done, Dean, but you know the rules. You're outta here. Send in the next brother."

Dean rose, still dripping cum, and grinned and waved to the camera before he fled. He left behind a shaking star. His gigantic thighs still in the air, his big butt spread wide, his hole painted with frothy spittle and now finally starting to pout open, all were a sight to see!

"Strip, Christoph. It'll be hotter if we're naked too."

The camera swung his way briefly as the next challenger appeared from the stairway. Christoph obeyed, allowing the tall art student to believe he was in charge. He tore off his tank top and stepped out of his sweatpants. A competitive swimmer, his lithe amber-brown body was smooth and muscular.

"Nice tool. Too bad you won't be able to use it on our star here tonight!"

Christoph's cock stuck straight up, a creamy-chocolate pole of prodigious length. He was understandably proud of it and glanced at Beau for a reaction, but the giant football player had his eyes on the approaching challenger.

While that frat brother settled in for his feast, Gabriel quickly handed off the camera to Christoph and tore off his own clothes. Long and lean, he was so tan his skin was almost darker than Christoph's, except where his sweet round ass gleamed white. His cock bobbed eagerly between his slender thighs as he took back the camera and continued filming.

The three challengers that followed placed Beau in three different positions, all nastily exciting. He lay on his belly with his giant ass rearing up from the bench with a contestant kneeling between his splayed thighs and his eager face rooting like a pig for truffles, snorting and slurping. Then the giant jock was placed on his hands and knees. His massive tits hung down between his shoulders and the challenger who licked up and down his crack also reached forward to tweak and tug at his nipples while he ate butt.

That got some good reaction and points were scored. Beau's kneeling body lurched while he hung his head down and practically blubbered.

The third of those contestants had the football star get up on the bench in a squat. That position showed off the width of his enormous back and shoulders, the girth of his thighs and calves and the massive size of his butt.

The hole itself gaped open between those squatting thighs, flaming pink and drooling spit. The lips were swollen and wracked with little spasms. The moment a tongue strummed across them, the beefy jock's humongous body lurched violently and he pushed back toward it with a loud groan.

The first two of these three challengers actually managed to time out, abandoning their sucking ass-meal after fifteen minutes were up. The third lasted less than five minutes, his tongue twirling up between those drooling butt-lips from behind as Beau squatted over his face and wriggled over that invading appendage. The challenger gave a gurgling cry as he spewed a load all over the bench between Beau's big thighs.

"I guess it's my turn. Take the camera, Christoph."

He did as he was told, pleased with the progress of his plot so far. Filming Gabriel eating out that jock butt would be a good insurance policy against any future recrimination. It was all going according to plan!

Still, he hadn't counted on Beau's amazing reactions or imagined how incredibly exciting it would be to watch him get sucked inside out.

"Stay like that. You're wide open for a good tongue-reaming," Gabriel ordered as he knelt behind the squatting football player and began to eat ass.

Christoph took a deep breath to steady himself as he aimed the camera and filmed. The night was muggy with the threat of an approaching tropical storm, and the floodlights were hot too. Beau's naked body glistened with sweat. It ran down the deep divide of his muscular back and into his mammoth ass. His mop of red hair was damp and tangled.

Down on his knees, Gabriel was dark tan against the pale backdrop of the big jock. His raven-black hair contrasted sharply with the flushed ivory of that colossal butt. His lean frame was about 120 pounds shy of the football player's hefty girth. Still, he took control immediately.

That was when Christoph entertained his first suspicions of the pair's complicated relationship, and his own perceptions of what had really gone on a year earlier when the football jock had been so keen to haze him in particular during pledge week.

Meanwhile, Gabriel seized the clenched mounds of that mighty ass and pulled them even wider apart as he shoved his face up into the spread crack and licked at the distended hole. He slapped those hefty cheeks and left them flaming pink. He nipped at the swollen lips and then buried his tongue between them.

The kneeling senior next did something none of the other challengers had yet dared. He reached up between Beau's thighs and pulled down his stiff cock. He wrapped his lips around it and sucked it deep.

Cock-sucking was not against the rules, but it didn't get you any points either. Except in this case, Beau's reaction certainly racked them up for the slurping art student.

The behemoth jock dropped his head between his gigantic shoulders and reared both backward and downward. His entire body heaved and writhed.

Gabriel licked along the shaft, down to his balls and into the crack of his ass.

All the while he was aware of the camera aimed at him and did his best to play for it. He moved his face aside so that Christoph could film the flushed wet hole, he sucked loudly and smacked his lips dramatically and even mugged for the camera, winking and grinning and licking his wide glistening lips nastily before diving back in for more ass-chewing.

Of course Beau was a quivering mess by this time. It was definitely satisfying for Christoph to see the giant football star shaking and moaning and heaving all over.

But it was time for him to intervene. It looked like the

writhing jock was hot and bothered enough for the coup de grace. And Gabriel's turn at the table had expired.

"I'm up now, Brother."

The dark-haired senior rose from his knees and grinned into the camera, wagging his tongue and pumping his stiff cock. "Enjoy! That's one big butt to play with and one sweet hole to dine on!"

It was his turn. He handed off the camera with only a glance at the leering senior. His suspicions were growing and he was afraid he'd show it, so he avoided eye contact with Gabriel and moved quickly to take his turn at the plate.

"Get down on your knees, face in the pillows and that giant butt in the air."

He didn't bother hiding the triumph in his voice. By now he was pretty sure the jock was brainless enough not to really get what it was all about. Still, it was very satisfying to see the massive hulk scrambling to obey.

There it was, his for the taking. Beau sprawled out on the bench, face buried between the huge girth of his arms, enormous thighs spread, and that oh-so-huge butt wide open and defenseless.

The asscheeks were flushed pink and glistening with sweat droplets. The smooth crack was even brighter pink, and the swollen hole was practically on fire. Six frat brothers had taken their turns orally abusing it. It oozed spit. The lips pouted apart, the center gaping and snapping.

He crawled up on the bench behind Beau and seized those flushed buns. Slippery and solid, they were truly gigantic under his palms. The football jock actually moaned and wriggled that monster butt, obviously eager for more attention.

Christoph dove in.

He went right for that hole. His mouth settled over the

dripping pit, his lips attached to the rim and his tongue thrust deep.

It was awesome!

The hole was gooey and loose, allowing his tongue to stab beyond the rim and into the steamy interior. And even better, the lips actually pushed outward and sucked back at his delving tongue. The jock had become a total hole!

Smelling and tasting that sloppy jock hole had him momentarily forgetting all about his devious plots. He went wild, rooting and probing, sucking and licking, smacking and lapping.

Beau rolled his massive hips back and forth, his knees sliding farther apart and his hole churning with little convulsions as it alternated between sucking at his tongue and gaping wide for deeper penetration.

On the brink of losing himself in the throes of devouring that delicious ass-cavern, he rallied. He recalled how a year earlier he'd been bent over the chapter-house toilets, ass in the air, his own pert, chocolate-brown asscheeks stinging as Beau wielded that paddle. He recalled now how he'd noticed Gabriel out of the corners of his eyes, lurking in the doorway, a big smirk on his handsome face and his hand down in his sweatpants obviously pumping a hard-on.

Now it all made sense.

He reared up and, lunging forward, mounted the prone jock. He thrust with his stiff cock. It drove balls-deep in the slot.

If ever a hole was primed for a fuck, this was it. He felt that slippery rim part and gobble, the steamy innards swallow and yield.

"Yeah, Christoph! Ya'll fuck that big ass jock. Show us how much he likes a stiff chocolate dick up his lily-white ass!"

As Gabriel urged him on with nasty encouragement, Christoph was now certain his suspicions were well founded. He bent down over the jock under him and placed his spit-wet mouth directly against his ear and whispered.

"Tell me, Brother, last year during pledge week, who told you to single me out for the worst shit?"

Between loud grunts, eyelids fluttering wildly, the football player hissed out his answer. "Who do you think?"

Exactly! Gabriel was the ultimate manipulator!

Both he and Beau were merely dupes for the brilliant art student to toy with. His eager cock pumping in and out of the jock's wet and sloppy hole, he found himself breathless, shaking all over and too excited to care about any of it right now. He fucked.

Turning to grin into the camera, and with his secret knowledge closely held, he pounded that giant ass for all he was worth. Ramming in and out, slamming his lean brown hips into the sweaty, massive, jiggling white buttcheeks, he drilled the poor football jock so furiously his grunts and groans turned into one long helpless wail.

"Fuck me!"

He reached under Beau's raised belly and grabbed his stiff, leaking cock. The fat tube immediately jerked and lengthened under his pumping hand. Under him, the enormous jock had gone almost entirely limp, his thighs slid wide apart on the bench, his butt in the air, his face buried in his powerful arms. His hole had gone loose and gaping as it accepted the furious pounding with squishy surrender.

The giant jock spewed.

He wailed louder as his beefy body convulsed under Christoph. His gaping hole clenched at the swimmer's thrusting cock as he sprayed the bench with his spunk.

That did it for Christoph. The feel of the monster jock surrendering his load was all he needed. Victory, of sorts! He

pulled out of the snapping hole just in time to spray the quivering mounds with a sticky mess of cum.

"Perfect! Our 'Big-Ass Jock' coated with nut-juice! Well
done, Christoph. I think you've won our little contest."

After that they cleaned up together. The rest of the challengers
joined them, all naked of course. One thing led to another and
they ended the night with an impromptu cock-sucking contest
that Beau managed to win as he took two cocks in his mouth at
once, and he grinned happily when his dimpled chin was coated
with cream.

Christoph mulled it all over for the next few days. He'd been
planning on posting their little film on a few websites, anony-
mously of course, exposing the big jock for what he was, an
eager hole for use. But now that he knew the truth about pledge
week, he changed his mind. What would be the point? It was
really Gabriel who'd manipulated them all, then and even now.

Revenge? What did that really matter either? He realized
he'd been too concerned about his own injured pride and now
that he'd acted it all out with the nasty film, he also realized
Beau was not really so different from him.

And the same for Gabriel. All three were a little on the arrogant side. It was Beau who was actually the most innocent of
them all. Gabriel had been manipulative, but not really any
more so than Christoph himself.

So after all that self-examination, he posted an edited version
of the clip.

Gabriel was on his knees chowing down on big, white,
anonymous ass. The handsome senior mugged and smirked and
licked his lips for the camera, then got back in for more hole-
diving and cock-sucking.

Of course when the art student was made aware of the clip by
a few grinning freshman, he wasn't the least bit angry. In fact,

he called Christoph into the chapter house office and offered him the vacant vice-president's position.

It was then Christoph realized the ultimate truth. Revenge is pretty much a waste of time—except, maybe, when it ends up in a hot ass-eating contest!

THREE LITTLE
LAMBS

Neil Plakcy

Larry Leavis walked past the Lambda Lambda Lambda table at rush week three times before he finally got up the nerve to stop and pick up a brochure. There were two guys behind the table: a gorgeous blond preppy in an Izod shirt and plaid Bermuda shorts and a Chinese-American guy with straight black hair and skin so smooth Larry wanted to reach out and touch it. They were busy talking to a buff Jamaican guy with dreadlocks, so Larry stood there awkwardly, looking at the pictures of the guys studying, playing touch football or hanging around the living room of the frat house.

They were all too good-looking, he thought. Nobody at the Three Lambs would ever even look at him. He'd always been a scrawny beanpole, taller than everyone else in his class, and though he'd begun to fill out in college, he still thought of himself as skinny and awkward.

He stuffed the brochure in his pocket and turned away. "Hey, wait," the preppy guy said, breaking away from his conversation. "I'm Fitz. You interested in Three Lambs?"

Larry looked down at the table and mumbled, "Yeah."

Fitz stuck his hand out. "What's your name?"

Fitz's hand was cool and his grip was strong. Larry felt a flutter at the pit of his stomach. "Larry," he said. "Larry Leavis."

"Cool. We're a new frat—this is our first rush. The house opened last year with just a half-dozen guys, though we've got room in the house for twelve." He opened another copy of the flyer and pointed at the modern-style house. "An anonymous gay benefactor bought the land and paid for the construction, to create a support network for GLBT students at FU."

Florida University was a branch of the state university system in southwest Miami. Larry had felt swallowed up by the huge student body. He hadn't made many friends, just focused on studying and getting good grades. When he had free time he ran along the track at the football stadium or worked out in the gym.

He smiled. "It looks nice," he said.

"You've got a great smile," Fitz said. "You should smile more."

Larry felt himself blushing. "Is everybody in the frat—you know—gay?"

Fitz nodded. "That's the idea. It's kind of like a safe zone, where you can be who you want to be without worrying about bullying or name-calling. It's like, really important, you know?"

Larry couldn't imagine anyone bullying the handsome blond, or calling him any name other than some romantic endearment. His polo shirt clung to his chest like a second skin, and he was as handsome as a male model. "We're having a get-together tonight," Fitz said. "At the house, at eight. Why don't you come over?"

"Okay," Larry said shyly. He looked at his watch. "Shit, I've got to get to class."

Fitz took his hand again, and and said warmly, "I hope we'll see you tonight."

Larry's heart raced as he took back his hand. "Sure, yeah." He turned and rushed down the sidewalk toward the math building, only then realizing that his dick was tenting his shorts like a flagpole. Oh, god, had Fitz seen that? How embarrassing. He couldn't remember popping a boner like that in public since the time he snuck into an X-rated bookstore in downtown Miami when he was a high school junior. He swung his backpack in front of him and tried to concentrate on math problems.

The Three Lambs house was just off campus, a couple of blocks from the freshman dorm, and Larry walked over there a few minutes before eight, excited and nervous. He'd never been to any kind of meeting of gay kids before; hell, he hadn't even come out to himself until he was at FU. At eighteen, he was still a virgin in every sense of the word—the only time he'd ever been naked in front of anyone else had been in gym class, and then he'd been so focused on not popping a boner that he'd been scared to look around him.

His hand shook as he pressed the doorbell. A moment later the door popped open and the Chinese guy said, "Hey, come on in. You're Larry, right? I'm Chuck. Everybody's in the living room." He pulled Larry in for a hug, and as the slim boy's body pressed against his, Larry popped another boner.

Larry was reeling. It was the first time anyone had ever hugged him other than aunts or uncles. Certainly the first time any guy as cute as Chuck had done so. He followed Chuck numbly into the living room, where a half-dozen guys were standing around talking. "What do you want to drink?" Chuck asked. "We've got Coke, Mountain Dew, Red Bull. I think we've even got some lemonade if you're, like, totally not into caffeine."

"Coke is good," Larry said, fumbling for the words. He couldn't believe he was in a room full of gay guys just like himself. It was awesome.

Well, they weren't all just like him. They were all kinds of good-looking, from the total buffness of a guy who looked like he played football; to the slim, wiry Chuck; to that Jamaican guy he'd seen at the table.

Chuck introduced him around, but Larry was too nervous and too conscious of his stiff dick to pay much attention to names. The football player was the last to be introduced, and Larry forced himself to repeat the guy's name. "Hi, Ryan," he said.

"Hey." Ryan leaned so close Larry could feel the guy's five o'clock shadow brushing against his ear. "Don't worry about popping wood, dude. We're all in the same boat."

Larry recoiled in shock, then looked down at Ryan's crotch. Sure enough, his dick was pressing against his jeans. Ryan saw him look, then look back up. He laughed, and for the first time Larry felt comfortable.

Chuck and Fitz talked about the frat's activities. They studied together, helping each other out with tough subjects. They played flag football and did volunteer work at an AIDS hospice. "But mostly we're focused on school," Fitz said.

"What about—you know," Ryan asked.

"What?" Fitz asked.

Ryan blushed, and Larry felt like he had to help the guy out. "I think he means sex," he said.

The possible pledges giggled nervously. "We're a very sex-positive house," Fitz said. "You want to have sex? Feel free. Just respect the other guys. Keep it in your room and clean up after yourself and your partner." He reached over and took Chuck's hand. "Chuck and I are a couple, but our relationship is open. You can do whatever works for you, without any judgment."

The meeting broke up a little later, everyone getting information about pledge week activities. Larry felt all the soda coursing through him and asked if he could use the bathroom before he walked back to the dorm.

By the time he was finished the other guys had left; only Chuck and Fitz remained. "So what do you think?" Fitz asked. "You want to join us?"

"I've never, um," he said. He meant to say, never thought about a gay frat, but instead said, "I've never actually had sex."

"Wow," Fitz said. "A good-looking guy like you? Were you really closeted in high school?"

"I'm not, like, cute or anything," Larry said. "I mean, there were other gay kids in school but they wouldn't look at me."

"They just didn't know what to look for." Fitz reached over and squeezed Larry's bicep. "You're strong, dude." He ran his hand over Larry's chest, and Larry thought he might faint from the pleasure. "Buff chest, too."

"And you've got a totally cute bubble butt," Chuck said, coming up behind him. He cupped Larry's ass, and Larry let out a big sigh. His dick was so hard he thought it was going to burst through his pants at any minute.

He was so focused on Chuck's hand on his ass that he didn't realize Fitz was leaning in to kiss him until the blond's face was right up against his. He didn't even get time to wet his lips before Fitz was kissing him, soft lips pressing against his. Fitz's tongue penetrated his mouth as the blond wrapped his arms around Larry. He smelled like sweat and lemon.

It was all so overwhelming. Behind him, Chuck was kissing the nape of his neck, his hand still cupping Larry's ass. He didn't even have his clothes off yet and already sex was better than anything he had imagined.

Fitz backed away, and Larry wanted only to pull him close again. "Are you cool with this, dude?" Fitz asked. "We don't want to make you do anything you don't want to do."

Larry almost laughed. "Are you kidding? You guys are both, like, so..." He couldn't even finish the sentence.

"You're pretty so yourself," Fitz said. "Come on. Let us show you our room."

Fitz took his left hand, and Chuck took his right, and they walked across the living room to a hallway and then into a big bedroom with a king-sized bed, two desks and two dressers. "*Nuestra casa*," Fitz said. "*Bienvenidos.*"

"Fitz is taking Spanish this term," Chuck said.

Fitz began kissing Larry again, as he slowly unbuttoned Larry's shirt. Chuck squatted down and ran his hand over the crotch of Larry's jeans. Larry shivered, closed his eyes and gave himself up to the pleasure.

As Fitz slipped Larry's shirt off, exposing his buff, hairless chest, Chuck began unbuttoning Larry's jeans. Larry and Fitz were still kissing, and Larry's dick was harder than it had ever been before. He felt like he was going to explode at any minute.

Fitz kissed his way down Larry's chin to his neck and then his right nipple. God, Fitz was sucking his nipple, then nibbling at it. It was like an electric current ran direct from there to his dick. He was so overwhelmed that as soon as his dick was out in the air with one of Chuck's smooth hands wrapped around it, he shot off, the cum arcing out like a rainbow.

Larry blushed furiously as Chuck and Fitz both laughed. "Dude, that's like a record," Chuck said. "Fastest cum ever."

"And farthest shot," Fitz said. "Look how far it went."

"I'm sorry," Larry stammered.

"For what, dude?" Fitz asked, as Chuck swirled his tongue around the tip of Larry's dick, licking away the last drops of cum.

"For, you know, coming so fast."

"Dude, we're only getting started," Fitz said, and he bit down on Larry's nipple.

Larry shivered and inhaled, throwing his head back, and he felt dick start to stiffen again. Maybe Fitz was right.

In short order, the three of them were naked, lying on the king-sized bed. Chuck lay on his back, and Fitz positioned Larry so he could suck the Chinese boy's dick. Larry had never sucked a dick before but he found it came naturally—he just opened his mouth and chowed down.

Meanwhile, Fitz had positioned his ass at Chuck's mouth, and Chuck was rimming him noisily. His stiff dick, surmounting a bush of dark blond pubic hair, wagged in front of Larry as he sucked Chuck. Larry reached up and grabbed it, jerking the blond with his own precum. Fitz groaned. "Oh, yeah, that feels so good."

As he got more accustomed to the idea of having a dick in his mouth, Larry began experimenting, sucking just the head of Chuck's dick, then licking up and down the shaft, even rubbing his chin against it. His five o'clock shadow made Chuck groan and squirm.

He felt Chuck's dick stiffen in his mouth and suddenly his throat was filled with hot, salty cum. He coughed and pulled back. "Sorry, dude," Chuck said, stopping his rim job on Fitz's ass. "Should have given you some warning."

"It's okay," Larry said, between coughs.

Fitz reached over to the table next to the bed and pulled a condom in a neon-green package out of the drawer. He tossed it to Larry. "Suit up, dude. Chuck's got my ass nice and wet for you."

Larry's mouth dropped open. The gorgeous blond wanted Larry to fuck him? Fitz's hair was matted to his head with sweat. He pulled off Chuck and positioned himself doggy-style on the bed, presenting his ass to Larry.

"I don't..." Larry began.

"Oh, right." Chuck scrambled off the bed and came over to Larry. He took the condom package from Larry's hand and tore it open. Then he squatted down in front of him. He licked Larry's dick, then pulled the condom down over it.

The sensation was uncomfortably tight, but he was so excited about getting to fuck his first ass that it didn't matter. Chuck pushed and tugged him so that he was positioned in front of Fitz's ass, even pulling apart the blond's asscheeks so Larry could slide right in. "Go on, go for it, dude," Chuck said. "He wants it. Don't you, Fitz?"

"Fuck my ass, pledge," Fitz said. "That's an order."

Larry rammed his dick into Fitz's ass, and the blond boy yelped. "Oh, fuck! Slam that dick into me, man."

Larry obliged. Chuck got behind him and began licking and fingering Larry's ass as Larry plowed his dick up Fitz's chute. They were all sweaty by then, and Larry kept losing his grip on Fitz's asscheeks. He felt like he was a cowboy up on a bucking bronco as he slammed his dick into Fitz over and over again.

He felt Chuck's finger behind him, snaking up his tunnel and scraping his prostate, and he lost it, just totally went ape shit, howling like a mad monkey, his dick spurting into the condom. As soon as the orgasm passed, he slumped against Fitz, who collapsed to the bed. All three of them were tangled up together in the sticky, sweaty sheets.

Fitz's dick was still stiff, and Larry realized he hadn't come yet. Fitz hoisted himself up on the bed, so that both Larry and Chuck were level with his dick. Chuck leaned in and started to suck—then backed off. "Your turn, dude," he said.

Larry looked at him. "Okay." He leaned in and started to suck the tip of Fitz's dick. Then Chuck attacked his boyfriend's balls, licking and sucking them, as Fitz moaned with pleasure. It was wild, being nose to nose with Chuck as both of them ministered to Fitz. Every now and then Chuck would pull off Fitz's balls and kiss Larry, both of them rubbing their heads against Fitz's flat belly.

Fitz started moaning and pleading to be finished off, bucking his hips against their mouths, and then with a yelp he spurted down Larry's throat.

This time Larry was ready, and he sucked every bit of cum from Fitz's softening dick. Then he sprawled on his back next to Fitz, Chuck on the other side. "This was..." He stopped, searching for the right word. "Awesome."

"Yeah, it was, wasn't it?" Fitz said, still panting. "So, have we convinced you to join Three Lambs?"

"It's not all fun and games, though, dude," Chuck said, leaning up on his elbow. "We study, we belong to clubs and we do volunteer work. All that stuff we said in the meeting."

"As long as we get to sleep sometimes," Larry said. "I am totally wiped."

"Snooze on, dude," Chuck said, and the three of them nestled in the big bed and went off to dreamland together.

THE PICKUP GAME

C. C. Williams

Jerry Gresham loved playing basketball.

I loved watching him. So we did that almost every day: he on the court beside the Lambda Chi house and I from my dorm room in Mason Hall. Daily I would sit at my desk, supposedly studying, but actually gazing entranced as Jerry and his fraternity brothers played hoops. My second-story vantage afforded a great view across the small grassy commons to the playing area with its lone netless basket. Jerry and his friends would play half-court, stripping off their shirts as they jostled and struggled for control of the ball. Studying forgotten, I would sit and watch, rubbing at my growing erection as I imagined Jerry's sweat-slick body under my hands.

If I was lucky, I could get a load off before my roommate Max came back from class. If not, I'd zip up and return to my books, willing my aching and unfulfilled cock to relax. Not that Max didn't know what I was up to: a couple of times I'd not heard him approaching and he had shown up at the crucial moment.

The first time he made a hasty exit; the second time he offered to help. So Max was cool, but not what I was looking for.

After a while, Max realized what was so fascinating outside my window.

"Jerry Gresham? You mean Mister 'so cool that every chick on campus wants to bang him' Gresham?" Max shook his shaggy hair, wondering at my stupidity. "Noah, Noah, Noah. Why not crush on someone totally unavailable—like that actor, Robert Pattinson? Now he's hot!"

I threw my hands up. "I don't know why!"

Actually I did, but I didn't want to sound as shallow as I felt. I had the same reason as every coed on campus who flirted with him: he was gorgeous. Golden-haired, tall and muscled, tan and totally fuckable—he was an absolute Adonis. And I wanted him—not because we were soul mates or destined to be together, but simply because he was hot, hot, hot.

My base desire warred with my sense of who I was. I wanted to be loftier, appreciating someone for who he was as a person, not for solely how well his genes had meshed together. But my libido was winning: all I could think about was Jerry—usually with no clothes on.

My problem was that we existed in different circles—the social strata of a small Midwestern college being similar to those in most high schools. Although Jerry wasn't academically challenged and I wasn't athletically inept, we were worlds apart—he was a fraternity jock and I wasn't. More than a little patch of grass separated us.

Max, as usual, got directly to the heart of the matter. "You either have to tutor him in physics or you have to play basketball. And basketball is sexier."

"Huh?"

"Play basketball with him! I know you've played!"

"That was in junior high school and only because I was the tallest eighth grader!"

"Nonetheless, it allows you to approach him on common ground where he's comfortable."

"What the hell? Are you channeling Dr. Phil?"

"I'm just giving you some advice, so you can stop whacking off at the window."

He even went so far as to give me a brand-new Wilson basketball; he called it a 'dorm warming' present. As much as I hated to admit it, Max was right: I could either make something happen or not—Jerry Gresham was not going to show up at my door of his own accord.

I took my ball and started shooting hoops. The ring of the ball echoed off the brick walls as I dribbled around the asphalt court. The thump of the ball on the plywood backboard chased the echoes around the commons. Awkward and rusty, I grew more confident as I practiced; jump shots, rebounds, even an occasional three-pointer, each regained a place in my repertoire. Sweating, I jumped and shot, over and over again, and remembered how much I had actually enjoyed playing.

The days passed. I focused more on putting the ball in the basket and less on hooking up with Jerry.

"Hey!" A voice pulled me out of my concentration, tearing me away from the basket and the free throw I was lining up. Wiping sweat from my forehead, I shaded my eyes against the afternoon sun. Jerry Gresham stood on the grass, holding a ball on his hip. The low sun cast an aura around him, pouring golden light over his bronze body.

My lungs stopped working.

"You wanna play?" His voice, rough and deep, rumbled across me. He released the ball and began to dribble as it rebounded.

I forced my lungs to work, dragging air into them. "I...I'm not very good."

"Bullshit! I've been watching you."

"You...you have?" All my saliva went away; it was hard to swallow.

"For a while." The fraternity boy dribbled closer, circling me. "I'm Jerry."

I turned, following his movements. His emerald-green eyes drew me in as he bounced the ball from hand to hand. I was in a trance—everything seemed hyperreal, yet distant from me. I felt like a spectator in my own body.

"I...I'm Noah."

"Yeah, I know." He passed the ball behind his back. "Come on! We'll even use your ball; it's better than mine anyway." He tossed his ball over his shoulder; it rolled away into the lengthening shadows. "Let's play!"

Jerry made a grab for the ball, but my brain and body reconnected in time for me to turn and dribble downcourt. Jerry shadowed me—he guarded well. We danced around the court, feinting and dodging, until I caught him with his weight wrong and drove around him to the basket. Two points! The game was on!

Jerry recovered the ball and headed downcourt. I guarded him, gauging his movement with the ball and looking for any offensive weakness. Skillful, he handled the ball comfortably with either hand. I watched his eyes, reading what they could tell me. Honestly, I just wanted to fall into their green depths.

Jerry glanced to the right, breaking my concentration just enough to move around me and head for the board. Damn! He was good! I ran after him, trying to get ahead in order to block him. Jerry drove in for a layup and smoothly delivered the ball through the hoop. The score was tied.

I snagged the ball and dribbled to half-court. Jerry stayed with me, keeping tight to my position. This time his weight was better distributed and I was hard pressed to catch him off balance. Unable to get past him, I went for a jump shot. The ball arced gracefully toward the basket only to bounce off the rim and careen back toward us. Jerry intercepted the rebound and dodged past me.

I caught up and kept with him, not letting myself get distracted. We wove around each other, moving more as a unit than as competing parts. Jerry would quickly change directions, never losing control of the ball, but I shadowed him, managing to stay tight as he shifted and dodged. Jerry went for the jumper. Unable to block his shot, I watched as the ball sailed cleanly through the hoop. Jerry four, Noah two.

Jerry signed a *T* with his hands. "Time-out," he panted. Letting the ball roll, he paused, bent over with his hands on his knees. As he straightened up, he grasped his T-shirt and pulled it off over his head.

I stared.

Hard and tan, Jerry's torso glowed in the afternoon light. His chest was wide, flat planes of muscle dotted with dark nipples. A dusting of fine golden hair covered his chest and drifted across his six-pack abs. The light fur narrowed to a thin line that trailed over his navel and down into his board shorts, which hung from his narrow hips. I wanted to follow that trail with my tongue.

Seemingly unaware of my lustful scrutiny, Jerry mopped sweat from his face and neck with the balled-up cloth. Tossing the T-shirt aside, Jerry loped after the ball.

"Damn! You are good!" He passed me the ball and grinned. Framed by two dimples, his perfect teeth flashed white. "How come you're not on the team?"

Dribbling, I slowly circled him and shrugged. "I've never tried out."

"You should." He shuffled sideways, staying between me and the basket. "You'd see some game time."

"Not really my scene." I feinted left. "I like one-on-one better." I darted right and made for the goal, Jerry hot on my heels.

The fraternity boy bore down on me as I neared the basket. I went for the layup. Jerry stretched to block the shot. My feet left the ground. His momentum carried him into me, knocking me sideways. Arms tangled, we fell, tumbling, to the ground and rolled to a stop, chest to chest, behind the basket. Jerry's weight pressed me into the grass.

Groaning, I opened my eyes. Jerry's face hung above me, backlit by a security light. *When had they come on?* I could smell him—a mix of sweat and something fresh, woodsy. My heart raced, pounding at my ribs like it wanted to get out. Jerry's skin burned against mine. Sensations flooded over me, swamping my brain. Time attenuated; my pulse pounded in my ears like a bass drum.

I drew a rasping breath, moving to get up. "I'm...uh...okay. Are you?"

Jerry leaned forward and pressed his mouth to mine. The touch stopped my breath in my throat. His lips, lush and insistent, sought to consume mine, demanded their attention. Bright sparks of pleasure shot along my nerves. My body tingled and responded of its own accord, arching against his, returning the urgency of the kiss.

I reached up, entwined my fingers in his silky curls and pulled his body down against me. My mouth strove against his. Suddenly his tongue was dancing with mine; wet and warm, it explored my mouth. I stroked my tongue across his teeth, felt the roughness of his tongue. His mouth sucked at mine greedily and tasted of sugar and mint.

Jerry broke away from the kiss. Taking a deep breath, he arched back to look down at me. "Oh, my god! I've wanted to do that for so long!"

My brain locked up...again. "You...what?"

"I've wanted to kiss you since we were in physics class last semester." Jerry rolled off of me on to his right side, resting his head on a fist. "You always sat three rows in front of me, next to Max. I was so jealous—I thought you two were together." He reached out and traced a finger along my jaw line.

"I...uh...you and...uh...Bekka..."

"Bekka Meiers and I grew up together! She's like my sister; she was actually the first person I told I liked boys." He draped his left leg over mine. "So we complement each other: I keep guys away so she can focus on getting into med school; she keeps girls away so I don't have to fake stories for my fraternity brothers."

My mental cogs had begun to loosen up. "So you're really bi? 'Cause Allyson Jackson says she's slept with you."

Jerry threw back his head and laughed. "Allyson thinks she slept with me—she wanted to, but she actually passed out first. I've just never denied it. But, no, I'm not bi. Guys are my thing—you're my thing."

To press home that point, he rubbed his groin along my thigh. He was rock hard under his baggy shorts—and not small either. I was responding the same way: painfully erect, my hard-on was trapped in my jockstrap. I reached down to adjust.

Jerry's hand landed on top of mine and pressed, gauging the evidence of my attraction. "Guess I'm your thing, too."

To answer him I leaned over and drew him into another embrace, less urgent than before, but no less intense, and we rolled on the grass. The shadows held us as we kissed; the basketball goal, long forgotten, stood sentinel as we moved against each other.

Again Jerry broke away. "I want you—all of you. But this is not where I want you." Rising to his knees, he drew me up. "I know a place that's more comfortable—and private."

Recovering his shirt and ball, he led me across the grass toward the Lambda Chi house. Skirting the side of the house, we paused at the back on an unevenly bricked patio strewn with beer cans. A whiff of stale vomit curdled the air.

"Oh, this is really charming."

"Shh!" Jerry held a finger to his lips. "We're just stopping so I can grab some stuff. I'll be right back." With that he slid open the patio door and disappeared into the fraternity house.

Alone in the night with my thoughts, I considered the chance this was a dream or, worse yet, some practical joke. If this were a prank, then Jerry Gresham deserved an Academy Award—because that was some kiss and a really big boner. Maybe I'd hit my head when we fell. I was possibly hallucinating, living out my dearest fantasy in my head. I pinched myself. It hurt. But I didn't wake up.

I recalled our kiss, how insistently his lips had pressed against mine, how sweet his tongue tasted as it explored my mouth. I closed my eyes, remembering the feel of his hair on my fingers as I pulled his toned, damp body against mine. I started to get hard again.

"You okay?"

I jumped, my heart jack hammering into my throat. "Holy shit!"

Jerry stood beside me, a duffel bag slung over his shoulder. "I thought you'd dozed off. Sorry I took so long." He put a hand on my shoulder. "God, you're beautiful. I can't believe I had the nerve to kiss you like that."

"I'm glad you did. I couldn't have been that bold."

"I was scared shitless." His hand gently massaged my shoulder. "I've never kissed a guy like that before. You know... without knowing if he wanted me to."

"Well, I wanted you to." I rubbed my cheek against his hand. "It was a good kiss."

"Honest?"

"Well, actually, it was a reee-ally good kiss." I grinned up at him sideways. "Best one I've ever had."

"Then we hafta have more. Come on!" Grabbing my hand, he led me through a gate and we headed across campus.

We ran down paths and across lawns, passing the student union and the admin building. Here and there we passed other students, none of whom seemed to notice that I was being towed along by Jerry Gresham. My fears began to rise again. I stopped.

"Hold up, Jerry."

He turned back to look at me. "What is it, Noah?"

"Is...is this some sort of prank?" I took a deep breath and rushed ahead. "'Cause, if it is, let's just call it good and be done with it. I'll leave you alone and we can pretend that none of this ever happened."

"What are you talking about?" He moved closer. A whiff of something fresh and spicy, wafted past me.

"You...me...this," I waved a hand vaguely in the air. "Is it real?"

"You mean you think that this is some kind of joke?" His voice grew hard.

"I...uh..." The fears and emotion rose into my chest, choking me.

"You think I would tell you those things just to fool you?"

"Well, no...I hope not."

"Would I do this"—he cupped my face in his hands and kissed me hard and deep—"if I wasn't for real?"

"It's…just…" Tears prickled behind my eyes. I swallowed hard. "Nothing like this ever happens to me." I felt a tear roll down my face.

"Well." His voice softened. "Nothing like this has ever happened to me either." He brushed away the tear with his thumb. "But I hoped it would."

He kissed me again, a soft caress from his lips. That fresh, spicy scent drifted around me again. I realized he'd put on cologne when we stopped at the fraternity house. I felt foolish; the fear and dark emotions started to drain away, replaced by a growing anticipation of something more. I smiled.

He grinned back, flashing those dimples. "That's better! Now, come on! I'll show you how real this is."

We continued our trek across campus. It became clear that our objective could only be the Eliza P. Sherman Fine Arts building.

"Why on earth did we come here?" I asked, as we stood before a side door. I rattled the handle. "Everything is locked down."

Jerry reached into the duffel. "Yeah, and one of my big brothers is Professor Jackson's TA." He pulled out a ring of keys. "He has after-hours access and uses it for more than working on his MFA."

Selecting a particular key, Jerry unlocked the door and motioned me in with a wave of his hand. The hallway glowed an eerie red, the only light the EXIT sign over our heads. He pulled a large flashlight out of the bag and flicked it on, washing out the red with bright, halogen white.

"Where are we heading?" I whispered, but my voice sounded stark in the silent building.

"The life drawing lab," Jerry replied in a normal voice, walking down the hallway. "There's no need to whisper: security doesn't patrol inside this building; they only check the exterior doors. One of my—"

"Let me guess—one of your frat brothers works in the security office and found out the patrol routes."

"Right!"

"Sheesh! You Lambda Chi guys are like a spy network!"

"Hey, brothers take care of brothers."

We moved deeper into the building, following the bright beam. A heavy, expectant silence absorbed the sounds of our movement and the dark silent classrooms were like a foreign country, unfamiliar and vaguely threatening. At the life drawing lab, Jerry examined the double doors and picked a different key on the ring. Opening the door, he ushered me into the darkened room and reached to the side to flip up a row of electrical switches. Instead of light a mechanical whirring issued from above our heads.

"Wow!" I exclaimed. Looking up, I watched canvas screens roll back to reveal a glass ceiling.

Moonlight flooded the large room, falling from the skylights. Racks of art supplies lined the walls and a small kitchen area huddled in a dark corner. Occupying the bulk of the space, wooden easels and stools cast blue shadows across the floor. Resting amid this midnight forest, bathed in silvery light, a wrought iron bed dominated the center of the art lab.

Jerry had doused the flashlight and wended his way through the easels toward the king-sized bed. Dropping the duffel beside the bed, he reached in, drew out a blanket and sheets and proceeded to make up the bed. "See? Private and definitely more comfortable than my bunk or that twin bed you have in your room."

"And the lighting is pretty cool, too."

Jerry pulled off his shirt and drew me close, holding my hips. "And you look cool in it."

His lips met mine and he edged backward, drawing me with him. Falling back on to the bed, he pulled me down atop him. Our kiss intensified as his hands moved beneath my shirt to stroke along my spine. Strong fingers caressed and kneaded the muscles across my back. I shivered from his touch. Cool air danced across my skin, magnifying the heat of Jerry's hands. His body hair tickled against my stomach.

Leaving his lips, I kissed across his jaw to nuzzle below his ear, his pulse strong and fast beneath my lips, his breath panting past my ear. I licked him, following the artery down his neck, tasting sweat and the tangy residue of his cologne. I explored ridges and valleys as my mouth traced over his shoulder and down his chest. His nipple tightened under my touch, a hard nub pressing against the tip of my tongue.

"Bite me," he groaned.

I nibbled on the taut flesh.

"No, harder!"

Drawing him into my mouth, I clamped my teeth into his skin. With a sharp breath, he arched his body against me.

"Yes, oh, yes! Now do the other side!"

Moving across his chest, I rubbed my face through his light fur, reveling in his scent. His other nipple was erect, awaiting attention. No hesitation this time; I bit his flesh, hard. He buried his fingers in my hair and pressed my mouth to his chest.

"Oh, shit, yeah!"

My dick was rock hard, straining in my jock. I moved to ease my hard-on; Jerry's hand stopped mine.

"Let me take care of that." His voice was thick and husky.

Sitting up, he rolled me onto my back. I supported myself on my elbows as he knelt over me. His erection tented his shorts, thrusting toward me. Jerry grasped my pants and pulled them off, leaving my jock stretched across my aching dick. Tossing the shorts aside, he buried his face against my trapped cock and inhaled deeply.

"Mmm—you smell good. Better than I dreamed."

He lay with his head in my groin and caressed my stomach and chest, circled my nipples, rubbing and tweaking. My muscles quivered, jerking at every contact. I had never been so sensitive to someone's touch; it was like his fingers traced lines of fire across my skin.

I murmured, "The way it feels when you touch me—it's awesome."

"It's awesome touching you."

Jerry slipped a finger under the straps of the pouch and lifted, releasing my erection so it sprang upward. Wetting his lips with the tip of his tongue, he lowered his mouth to my cock. Warm and moist, he engulfed me, taking me to the base. I collapsed back on the bed, spreading my legs, waves of heat rolling across me as his mouth stroked the length of my cock. He swirled his tongue around my cockhead, teasing at the slit. My stomach quivered, my abs convulsing as sensations shot outward from my groin.

Jerry took my balls in hand, softly rolling them about in the sac. Meanwhile, a lone finger stroked beneath the taut straps, teasing the flesh along my thighs and between my ass and balls. Sparks shot along my nerves, firing the overwhelmed synapses again and again. Tugging gently on my nuts, he dragged me closer and closer to orgasm.

"I...I'm going to come."

"Good." I heard the grin in his voice. "I want to taste you— the real you."

His mouth increased tempo and pressure, adding more fuel to my burning desire. My nuts tightened, pulling against his fingers, as come pumped out of my cock. Digging my fingers into the sheets, I spasmed and jerked; load after load of sticky fluid shooting into Jerry's mouth. Lips clamped tight on my twitching cock, he struggled to swallow, inhaling through his nose to keep from gagging.

At last the convulsions subsided and Jerry threw himself beside me, wiping his mouth with the back of his hand. "Man! That was hot! You taste so great!"

I turned to him, gazing into the emerald depths of his eyes. "That was amazing—I've never felt like that before."

"Well, I could get used to feeling that!" He chuckled, a deep, rumbling sound.

I rolled nearer, settling my hand on the peak in his shorts. "Right now, I want to feel this!"

Reaching under his waistband, I grabbed hold of his erection. He filled my hand, a warm and silky tube of hard flesh. I could feel it pulsate as his heart pushed blood through the engorged vessels. The head was sticky with precome. Exploring lower, I ran my fingers through the bushy hair over his large testicles and encountered what felt like a series of metal rings in the skin of his balls.

"What the—?"

"They're called lorums." He placed a hand atop mine, holding it in place on his cock. "I had them done last spring break in New Orleans." Keeping pressure with his hand, he rubbed his hard-on against my palm. "It was on a dare."

"You lost?"

He snickered. "No, I won—by having them done."

"I see." The immediate surprise was wearing off and the idea now began to turn me on. I wanted to see them. Kneeling beside him, I pulled off his board shorts, along with his jock. His cock was magnificent; long, pale and fat, laced with blue veins, it thrust upward from his blond bush, a shiny string of precome dropping to his belly. And there at the base of his cock were three small metal rings piercing the skin at the top of his sac.

"Holy cow! Can I touch them?"

"Go ahead."

Each ring was the diameter of my pinky and they were placed one above the other so they overlapped slightly. I was enthralled. I had heard of such things but had never imagined seeing them in the flesh, so to speak. Lowering my head, I ran my tongue across the rings. The combination of metal and man taste stirred me, driving blood to my groin.

Jerry gasped.

I looked up. "You okay?"

Jerry grinned down at me. "Never better."

I returned to his dick, tracing the bloodlines with the tip of my tongue. Silky smooth, yet rock hard, the paradox of a man's cock enchanted me once again. I lapped at the head, tasting the saltiness of his precome. Jerry continued to breathe deeply and regularly, pacing himself as I kissed and gnawed at his hard-on. His scent drifted around me, sweaty and sharp, making my dick even harder. Again and again I moved down to the piercings to tickle them with my tongue.

Jerry groaned. "I'm going to come, but I want you inside me first."

"You...want me...inside you?"

Jerry had rolled over and was rummaging in his bag. "Are we going to play twenty questions every time we have sex?" He rolled back to face me, having retrieved a bottle of lube and pack of condoms.

"Uh...well...no."

"Good!" He hooked a thumb toward his chest, "Because I..." He pointed his finger at me, "want you..." He tossed me a foil square. "Inside me—now!"

Uncapping the bottle, Jerry squeezed a palm full of lube while I stripped off my jock. I tore open the packet and unrolled the latex, my cock twitching in anticipation as Jerry raised his legs. Spreading his cheeks, he applied the slick gel to his puckered ring and rubbed a good amount on the head of my cock. My cock was like a steel rod; I couldn't remember ever having been so hard.

"Come on, Noah, fill me up!"

He rested his legs on my shoulders, and I pressed down on my cock, positioning the head at his hole, and pushed forward. Jerry inhaled sharply. I paused, watching him grimace. His face relaxed and he urged me forward, pulling on me with his legs. Slowly I pressed against him and watched, entranced, as the head of my cock disappeared into Jerry Gresham's ass. Blowing out a long breath, he moaned, "Oh, yeah. Take me, Noah Armstrong, take me!"

Leaning forward, I breathed in as Jerry's warmth enveloped me. "You know my name." Taking my weight on my arms, I moved farther into him.

Jerry dropped his legs, wrapping them around my hips. "Noah Peter Armstrong, I know a lot about you."

Withdrawing slightly, I slid in again. "Such as...?"

His legs pulled on my hips, grinding his butt against me as his balls rubbed against my pubes. "I know your favorite color is green."

I pulled out slowly. "Mmm..."

He started to beat off, wetting his dick with spit. "You won a contest to get your physics scholarship."

I slid in, reveling in his velvety smoothness. "Mmm-hmm..."

Slowly he stroked his pale cock, saliva and precome shining in the moonlight. "You played basketball in junior high."

I circled my hips, moving my cock inside him. "How do you know all this?"

He stroked faster, rubbing his swollen cockhead. "Max was my physics tutor. I asked him."

Pulling out, I plunged in again, increasing my pace. "And why did you ask him?"

Jerry groaned, his ass tightening around me. His fist pumped, slapping against his belly. "'Cause I wanted…"

Faster and harder, I drilled his ass. My balls pulled up. "What did you want, Jerry?"

"I wanted you to—" he gasped. Semen shot across his chest; ropes of white fluid streaked his tanned torso, his abs spasming as his body pumped out seed.

I rammed into him. "Did you want me to fuck you?"

His ass clamped on my cock. I came, fire exploding through my guts, burning behind my eyes. My balls unloaded, filling the rubber.

Joined together, our bodies quivered and jerked. I collapsed onto his chest, burying my face in his neck

Jerry's arms enfolded me; he kissed my cheek and whispered, "I want you to love me."

Turning, I kissed his lips. "I'd say that makes the game a tie."

THE GREEK PRESIDENT AND THE FOOTBALL PLAYER

Bob Masters

Want another beer, man?" asked the tousle-haired boy holding the plastic cup filled to the brim with sudsy brew that spilled down the side.

"Sure, why not," answered James, as he took the proffered cup and proceeded to take a gulp while he surveyed the surroundings. It was rush night at Phi Kappa Sigma, and James Marston was feeling pretty good about it. It had been his third rush party for PKS. They held several throughout the first part of the school year, waiting for the week before homecoming to accept new pledges. The competition was fierce, and James was proud to have made it this far. No hazing for him yet. Two other rushing wannabes had wound up stripped and blindfolded earlier in the evening, diapers pinned around their private parts before they were put in a car and driven to the outskirts of town. James understood that they would be dumped a few miles out and would have to make their way back before dawn, wearing only those diapers the whole way. So far he had avoided anything like that. And this was his third rush, which had to mean something.

"Can I have your attention please!" a voice rang out above the noise of the drunken fraternity party. "Attention! Phi Kappa Sigma has business to attend to tonight." It was Richard Caxton, president of PKS house. He had a natural way of drawing attention, his handsome looks and dark hair easy on the eyes. James could not help but feel a twinge of anxiety. "We have one prospective pledge here tonight who has shown a strong desire to become a member of our noble fraternity."

A low rumble filled the room, the loud and more than slightly drunken frat boys seeming to come instantly to some kind of almost sober attention.

"James Marston is a suitable candidate for pledge status in every way. But he still has to learn a few more things about what it means to be a member of Phi Kappa Sigma. He needs to learn proper etiquette. Let us begin the etiquette ceremony. Members, take your places!"

About fifteen frat members lined up next to each other in a single line, shoulder to shoulder. James felt suddenly alone and very much the center of attention. He didn't realize that he was the center of attention to Richard Caxton, who was looking directly at him with an inscrutable expression on his face. He could not know that Richard was sizing him up, this pledge with his football-player physique and light blond hair. *It's this kind of boy who has popularity handed to him,* Richard thought as he mentally prepared to give the instructions. *They don't have to work the crowds and schmooze with idiots to get elected president. I do, but now that I am president of this fraternity, maybe I can do something extra to take this self-assured pretty boy down a peg or two.*

"The members will take off their shoes and socks. James is

to strip down to his underwear and don a blindfold. Then he
will get down on his hands and knees. He will proceed in this
manner down the line of members, pausing to kiss the feet of
each one until they tell him to move on. He will do this until he
reaches me, the president of Phi Kappa Sigma. I will give him a
final task. If he completes this challenge, he may be considered
for pledge status. Let the etiquette ceremony begin!"

James kicked off his shoes and socks while the rest of the
house did the same. He felt self-conscious as he undid his belt
and let his pants fall down around his ankles. His heart rate
increased as he unbuttoned his shirt and pulled off his T-shirt.
A boy walked over to him and placed a blindfold around his
eyes. Then he was led over to the first barefoot frat member in
line and gently pushed into kneeling position before him. James
lowered his head until he could smell the feet of the member. He
places his lips against what felt like the top of a naked foot and
smacked the naked flesh with a suppliant kiss. The boy said,
"Proceed!" and so James shuffled over to his left, feeling with his
hands for the next set of feet. This he did for the next fifteen sets
of feet, all the while working his way down to Richard Caxton.
He could not know that Richard was getting turned on by the
sight of the naked football player kissing the feet of his fellow
members. He could not know that Richard was planning on
upping the stakes a little, a prerogative of his office and his duty
as chapter president. The shots of whisky might be going to his
head just a little, but Richard grew convinced with each passing
kiss that it would be his pleasure to make the young man suck
on his dick. Not very long, no, just a few bobs up and down on
it, showing his willingness to obey. Yes, that would make him
understand who held the power here. He felt the blood rush to
his crotch as James grew closer. When the blindfolded muscle-
boy awkwardly stumbled down before Richard's feet, Richard

became enflamed with a sense of domination. He unzipped his fly and let his semierect penis flop out. He told James to raise his head and proceeded to slap his half-hard dick against the blindfolded cheek a few times.

"I want you to suck on this dick. You only have to show that you will, for a few seconds. It is your final test."

James could not believe what he was hearing. First the feet and now this... He let his mouth fall open and then felt the tip of a penis being shoved inside it. James panicked and inadvertently fell forward, driving the hardened shaft deeper into his mouth. He felt himself gurgle as the thick tool slid back and forth over his tongue, stretching his mouth so that his throat could feel the head of the tool poke against it. Fires of erotic pleasure erupted up and down his spine as he felt his own body respond to the lewd invasion of his oral cavity. Could it be that he was actually enjoying the feel of a hot stud's cock stretching his mouth open wide as the frat president plunged his engorged man-meat down his throat? The sounds of his squelching mouth and the cheering, drunken frat boys combined with the beery smells and taste of sex made James lose any reservations. He allowed himself to fantasize that he was a sexual superstar instructing the fraternity on how to give a fantastic blow job. He swallowed Richard's plunging cock and let his tongue flick and dart all around it while he made his lips pulse against the thrusting shaft, milking it expertly so that the arcs of pleasure would build imperceptibly into waves of orgasmic delight. Though he had never done this before, the techniques began to have the desired effect. He felt Richard grasp the back of his head and start face-fucking him so that his entire cock could drive all the way in and back out again, staccato fashion. It wasn't too long before sensations of pleasure built up in Richard's crotch to the breaking point. He shuddered in orgasm as spurt after spurt of erupting cum filled the mouth of the football boy. The boy, in turn, was shooting his own load inside his underwear, his mouth impaled on Richard's cock as his body shook with spasms of ecstatic release.

Richard leaned back and closed his eyes, thinking that this was not what he had expected; he had never intended to let himself get carried away like this. He was awoken from this reverie by the sounds of frat members shouting.

"Benny, what the hell are you doing!" and "Benny, you must be really drunk!"

Richard opened his eyes to see Benny, the wrestling team member who was always toadying up to him, had pulled James's underwear down and was getting ready to push his spit-slick-ened cock up his ass. Richard watched as Benny stupidly and drunkenly shoved his dick into James. The boy grunted and fell forward into Richard's legs. Feelings of shame and anger filled Richard suddenly. Benny has gone too far. He had to stop this. Richard pushed violently against Benny so that he flew off James, landing a few feet away, his head smacking hard against the wooden floor. Richard offered his hand to James, who grabbed hold of it. He lifted him up and said softly, "I am sorry for letting the ceremony go on too long. Please accept my apologies. Let me help you get dressed."

They walked together over to where James had left his clothes. Richard handed him pants and shirt as the boy got dressed. The party resumed with a slow rumble of confused and drunken avoidance of what had just transpired. Richard was taking control for them; they didn't have to deal with it. That was the way it should be. Richard led James to the front door. "We will be bidding on prospective pledges in the next few days. I will put in a good word for you. Good night."

With that the door was shut and James was gone. Richard

turned and walked up to his private room, the one perk as fraternity president that made all the hassle worth it.

The next morning, both boys woke up with a solid notion that more than just a drunken hazing incident had taken place the night before. But neither wanted to deal with the implications of what that might mean. James was convinced he would have to wait until the future to figure out why he had felt absolute pleasure in giving Richard Caxton a blow job. The only trouble was whenever he thought about it, his cock grew hard and his breathing labored. He realized that it was essentially an embarrassing and shameful act, doing that in front of all of those frat members. But even that kind of turned him on. No, he had better wait, he thought. Becoming a pledge to Phi Kappa Sigma was more important now. He could deal with sexual identity crises later.

Richard woke up with a hard-on too and he knew now there was a whole side of his nature that he had never suspected before. He had not expected that orgasm to occur. It just happened. And how could he ever explain his reaction to seeing Benny try to fuck James? He wanted to tell himself that he was just protecting the reputation of Phi Kappa Sigma. But he knew deep down that he had acted out of jealous rage.

Still, he hadn't become president of the chapter by worrying about little things like sex. And for him to suddenly appear gay would certainly hurt his popularity. The bidding process would begin today. He would have to squelch any rumors that might have started about last night. He was drunk and let the situation get out of control that was all. He left his room and went downstairs to get a cup of coffee. It was later than he thought and the bidding process was almost ready to start. He gulped down his coffee and ran back to put on a pair of jeans and polo shirt. He had to look the part of the frat president at all times.

"Let us begin the bidding process for Phi Kappa Sigma pledges," he intoned as the group of bleary-eyed and hungover frat boys struggled to look awake. The discussion began among them of the various candidates. Most had dropped out or had been rejected by the second rush party. There were one or two who were acceptable. The two from last night's party who were given the diaper treatment had never returned and so were ineligible. That brought the meeting down to the discussion of one James Marston.

"I...I...think that he showed too much weakness last night. He should have stood up for himself more. I don't think I want to bid for someone like that, who does whatever somebody tells them to do, even if the orders come from a fraternity." It was Benny, and he was not trying too hard to keep the note of hurt pride in his voice from showing. Benny was like that, Richard thought. Simple-minded, honest, but emotionally raw and volatile. Benny had idolized Richard ever since he had been made a member of the fraternity. He was built like a professional wrestler: short, squat, with bulging muscles topped by a swath of thick, black, curly hair. He always did stupid things like last night's antics. Now he was confused. Richard would have to use his skills in persuasion to get him to come over to James's side. He only now realized that he very much was on James's side. Benny had made him realize that he wanted James back in the house as a pledge very much.

"I think he showed initiative and respect for us by going through the etiquette ritual. What happened afterward is only due to the amount of alcohol we were drinking. I trust that no one's feelings got hurt. I let my desire to humiliate him go just a little too far. I think he has paid the price of initiation. I say we bid him for pledge status," said Richard with practiced declamatory style, keeping his language neutral, yet positive.

"Yes, I think we open ourselves up to disciplinary hearings if we let our hazing rituals get too alcohol-infused. I think we should bid for James to help soften any angry feelings he might have toward us as a result of last night's…well, assault is not the right way to put it, but there were certainly mitigating factors." That was Kenny, the absolute opposite of Benny. Where Benny was emotional and volatile, Kenny was cool and reasonable. He was double majoring in psych and prelaw. The frat could count on him to guide them in the right direction. He was super-smart and very nice. His statement just now would set the tone on how the frat would view last night's incident. It was not "an assault" but there were "mitigating factors." It would all be drowned in an alcoholic haze and Richard would never have to deal with it. *We watch each other's back here in Phi Kappa Sigma,* he thought. Kenny had seen the direction things were going and had helped resolve the confusion. In time, the conversation turned back to Benny, and Richard had to use his experience in dealing with Benny's need to have him as some kind of big brother he could idolize. Evidently the sex with James had shaken Benny's picture of Richard. That was not a problem; he just had to reassure him that the sex meant nothing, that his reaction to Benny's stupidity was nothing, that it all came from a bottle and that they would not drink so hard the next time. It allowed Benny to change his opinion and assent to letting James become a pledge.

Richard felt a little elation at winning the bidding process over to James Marston. He knew deep down inside him why he was feeling so happy about the outcome. But he also felt he had to deny himself any further enjoyment of James as a sexual partner. It was plain that he could never come out of the closet and keep his popularity and acceptance here at Phi Kappa Sigma. He would have to play the role of disinterested frat president, one who had hazed him and forgotten about it; it was all just part of the game. Richard asked Kenny if he would go tell James that he had been accepted as a pledge. Kenny dutifully said that he would and left. Richard was glad that he could deny the feelings of irrational excitement that thoughts of James brought out in him. He was good at closure, at ending things that might cause harm to his hard-won status.

James met Kenny at the door of his dorm room and almost fainted when he heard the news. He was now on the football team and a pledge at Phi Kappa Sigma. All of his plans for college life were coming true. The only part of the picture that he hadn't planned on was that the All-American player had a thing for Richard Caxton's cock.

A few hours later, James showed up at Phi Kappa Sigma with a small suitcase in hand. He would spend a week or two learning the rules and history of the fraternity while he stayed in a room with Kenny. Once he completed his duties and challenges as pledge, he would be inducted as a full-fledged member of PKS. Kenny had told him how Richard had fought for his acceptance as pledge. That made James more confident that he shared the same feelings that he did. But he would have to wait until he became a member before he told Richard anything about his feelings for him. Too much was riding on his following the rules. It might look like he was trying to get in by manipulating the president. He didn't want that. But Richard did look handsome and so sophisticated.

Richard was very happy that James was under the same roof as himself, but he actively tried to dampen down any further emotional exuberance he felt about him. He told himself he would have to investigate how the fraternity really felt about gay people and how they might react to someone like himself coming out of the closet all of a sudden. They had a right to expect their elected president to act a certain way. Everything was going according to plan all right, but seeing James walk around with Kenny and meet the other members made something tighten in Richard's chest. It wasn't fair that he had to pretend not to be interested in the boy. Besides, he had to show him how sorry he felt about the embarrassing position he put him in the previous night. So it was with every intention of simply getting him alone and somewhere quiet that Richard approached James as he was sitting with his nose buried in some thick tome of Phi Kappa Sigma history that he would supposedly have to answer questions about later.

"Hi there. Welcome to Phi Kappa Sigma. I see you are avidly studying the proper materials. Don't study too hard. I won't make the questions that difficult. Just the founding dates and things like that. No one but fanatics memorize all the stuff in between then and now," said Richard.

"Oh, thanks. I was wondering if I was going to be able to memorize all this and do all my homework next week. And it's going to be homecoming, were going to have a big game," said James.

"That's right; you're on the football team. That's great; we love to be represented in the college's football program. Say, I would like to get you away from all this hustle and bustle so I can talk to you about what happened last night. I am afraid things got a little out of hand and I would like to apologize. Come up to my room. I have the only private room in the house," offered Richard.

"That's cool. I don't remember much of what went on, but if you want to explain what happened, I'm open to listening. I don't want you or any of the others to get the wrong impression about me," said James, knowing full well that he remembered each and every detail of what happened, down to the last drop of Richard's cum.

The invisible bond between them led them upstairs to Richard's room where he closed the door and then turned to James.

"I am just really sorry about what I did to you last night, man. You shouldn't have been made to do that in front of all those guys," he said imploringly, his voice cracking just a little.

"Don't worry about it, Richard. I was a little drunk and confused, that's all."

"Hug? I want you to feel welcome."

They embraced and felt each other's warm bodies close against each other for the second time in less than twelve hours. Neither let go of the other. Their faces met. Then their lips. After a few minutes of selfless kissing, Richard reached behind him and turned the lock on his door. He took James by the hand and led him to his bed, throwing him softly down on the mattress and then lying on top of him. They ground their bodies together for several minutes, reveling in the smells and textures of each other. Soon their shirt buttons were undone and chests and nipples were being fondled and kissed, tweaked and set aflame. Belts became unfastened and pants and underwear pulled down. They needed only to rub their hardened cocks together for a few minutes while they kissed and hugged before both boys splattered the space between them with hot shooting spurts of white hot cum that glued them together. The sticky warmth filled both their nostrils and their minds as they fell silently asleep for a few minutes, basking in the glow of their newfound sexuality.

Richard awoke in a panic. He realized he had betrayed his promise to himself to keep these feelings under wraps.

"You have to keep quiet about what just happened. Promise me you won't mention this to anyone ever. Okay?" he said to James, a note of fear evident in his voice. He was up and getting dressed before James could even think of a response.

"Why do you want to keep things so quiet? You know it's

the first time I've done anything like this too. There are gay organizations on campus now, you know. It's not like we have to be ashamed," James finally answered, his ire growing with each passing moment as Richard hurriedly donned his clothes and began combing his hair.

"I know, I am not ashamed. It is just that things are different for me. I'm president of this fraternity. I can't let things get out of control. I have to look like I'm the same guy they voted for."

"I'm sure they'll understand. You have to admit that you brought me up here for more than just an apology. Even I was not quite that stupid."

"I know, I know. And I'm not saying we can never do it again. We just have to keep it quiet."

"On the down-low, you mean?"

"Yes, on the down-low, whatever, look, I have to go," and with that, Richard rushed out the room.

Asshole, James thought. He threw on his clothes and rushed from the room a few moments later. He had all kinds of emotions churning through him and needed to talk to someone about what had just happened. He saw Kenny sitting in the library room and walked inside.

"Kenny, can I talk to you about something?" he said, his voice breaking in spite of his best efforts to hide his feelings. Kenny picked up on his pain and asked him to sit next him.

"What's up?"

"It's Richard. He just had sex with me again and now he won't let me talk about it. I think I love the guy but I don't want to get hurt by letting myself get used as a sex object. I already allowed that to happen last night. I don't want it to keep happening. I don't know what to do."

"Ah, so my suspicions are correct. I knew that Richard exposed more of himself last night than he intended to. Today has been just one big denial. But it sounds like he might be able to come around, if you give it some time. He needs to feel safe."

Just then a figure stood up behind a study desk in the corner of the library room and rushed out before James or Kenny could stop him.

"I wonder if he heard. I wasn't supposed to tell anyone. I thought I could trust you, Kenny."

"Who knows who that was? You can trust me, but things might get a little interesting here in a few minutes."

Just then they could hear Richard's booming voice ring out from upstairs.

"I am NO FAGGOT!"

James looked at Kenny, the hurt showing plainly in his eyes.

"The only desire I ever had for that boy was to humiliate him, and I did a damn good job of that last night, didn't I?"

James turned to Kenny with tears streaming down his cheeks. The big football player looked pitiful, his lips beginning to quiver as he struggled to find words.

"I guess this means that my time here is over. I can't stay in a situation where I am going to be used and abused."

With that, James stood up and left, a strong resolve having taken over him after the initial shock of hearing Richard's disavowal. Kenny sat motionless for a moment, hearing just beyond earshot a continual harangue upstairs between Richard and Benny. Kenny felt a wave of anger pass through him. He stood up and walked upstairs to where the loud voices were coming from. There, in Benny's room, Richard was standing, red-faced and shouting, while Benny looked on with alternating expressions of rage and scorn. He had never seen Benny look so mean. Well, he was feeling kind of mean himself.

"The boy you love and who loves you is packing his things

right now. You better get your act together now, chump," he said. A confident expression covered the emotional turmoil that boiled inside him. He always had that talent, hiding the weakness to appear cool and collected. It worked for lawyers. It was convincing, if done well. And he had evidently pulled his act off for a bewildered look of fear and stunned amazement flashed on Richard's face. He then turned and ran from the room. Benny looked at Kenny. Kenny had had it with him as well.

"What is your problem, dickhead? Are all wrestlers as dumb as you?"

Richard ran as fast as he could to Kenny's room, but James was not there. Deciding he must be on the way out the door, Richard turned and ran downstairs, headed for the front foyer. He saw James boldly walking toward the doors and feared that the new pledge would not stop to listen to him. Instead he rushed past James and used his body to block the front door.

"Please forgive me, James. I've been acting a little crazy. I want you to stay with me. Even if it means moving away from here, I need you."

James stopped and looked at Richard. He looked overcome with emotion.

Richard fell to his knees. A crowd of frat members had followed the commotion and were now standing around in the foyer.

"I want everyone to hear this. I am gay—from the tips of my toes to the top of my head, and I don't care who knows it!"

James and Richard embraced.

"And you are welcome to stay here and live together," a voice from the foyer sounded in the hushed silence of onlookers. It was Kenny.

"Do you really mean that?" asked Richard as he turned his face to the crowd.

A resounding "Yes!" filled the foyer.

"Thank you all."

Richard was overjoyed that his obligation to the president's image could include being a football player's lover after all.

Later that night, after all the thanks and hugs and happiness, Richard and James were in bed. A knock sounded on their door. Richard got up and opened to find Benny standing there in his underwear.

"Can I come in?"

"Why sure, Benny, come right in. You sure are dressed appropriately."

"I know, tell me about it. I can't sleep. I think I might be gay too. The wrestling team is gonna kill me. What should I do? Can you two guys help me?"

"Is that what's bothering you, Benny? Why don't you sit here between me and Richard?" asked James.

"Oh, okay," he said, ambling over, his huge muscles rippling with each strategic step. The three did indeed sit there and discuss Benny's "homo problems" for a few minutes. But thigh was touching thigh and Benny's cock was sticking out his briefs. Richard went down on him while James sucked Benny's face.

"Would you like to finish what you started last night, Benny?" asked James as he turned over on his stomach and stuck his butt out.

"Only if Richard says it's okay."

"Only if I get to fuck you at the same time, Benny."

Benny licked his lips in anticipation.

"You don't know how long I've waited to hear that."

THE LAIUS
LEAGUE

Gavin Atlas

In your senior year, it was considered a dire humiliation to still be a Chrysippus, a bottom, in Timberlands University's secret society, the Laius League. However, if you ejaculated when a Laius, a top, fucked you, you remained a Chrysippus until you could control your need to submit. In truth, the League wasn't supposed to be about sex. You went into the Laius League for the deep connections you'd acquire for later in life—access to the corridors of power in New York, DC and all over the nation.

Timberlands was a small men's college in Tennessee, and just about everyone was straight, at least on the surface. Thus, the "elders," who were mostly made up of seniors and grad students, only got one shot at most of the Chrysippi—the vast majority passed the test on the first try. Unfortunately for me, they got as many cracks at my ass as they wanted because I can't help but shoot every time I'm fucked. I had to wear a silver ring inscribed with the Greek letter chi surrounded by vines that represented bondage. If a guy flashed me a gold ring with a lambda and a crown, I had to bottom for him, regardless of whether I had a class or any other kind of plans.

It was the end of spring semester, and I had one last chance to move up from Chrysippus to Laius. I was told by my mentor, Chaz, that it would be with him. He was a grad student who had fucked me at least twenty times. It was unfair how perfect his dick felt inside me. How was I supposed to keep from coming when I was shot through with euphoria every time he was inside me?

Chaz told me he'd see me after my last class as a college undergrad—a sociology class called Analysis of Alterity that was tacitly required for everyone in the Laius League. You weren't supposed to take it until you moved up from Chrysippus, but this was my last opportunity.

The instructor, Professor Whit, was sort of a nut. He was tall and powerfully built, and he had a Mark Twain mustache, but the most noticeable thing about him was his booming voice. More than one person has said that in a different decade he would have been a dictator brought to power by his immense cult of personality instead of a professor at a small college.

His first reading assignment for the class was *The Sneetches*, by Dr. Seuss, about creatures with stars on their tummies who thought they were better than identical creatures that had no stars. At the time I hardly cared about whatever lesson Dr. Seuss was trying to teach because I was entranced by Professor Whit's voice, his height, his mesmerizing eyes and the sizable bulge in his pants.

Despite my lust for the teacher, I did manage to hang on to the class. Barely. Alterity apparently means "otherness," and Professor Whit said the Seuss book showed that people naturally divide themselves into groups that don't get along. There's always "otherness."

Sometimes it's something you're born into. If you're white, you'll never completely know what it's like to be Asian or Black. If you're male, you can't totally perceive the female; even, and Professor Whit actually said this, men who let other men fuck them all the time. I remembered fidgeting and blushing, because it seemed like he was staring right at me as he spoke.

Professor Whit was ending the course by talking about alterity factors we do choose, like fraternities. You join Sigma Chi, and all of a sudden you've inherited an enmity for the Zeta Beta Tau boys next door when you had no quarrel with them the day before. But you make that choice because there is a need to belong.

I took furious notes, preparing for the final. But the discussion of fraternities had me reliving my initial hazing with the Laius League. Wearing only a pair of white briefs, I'd attended a party during which the Laius brothers looked me and the rest of the pledges over. That night Chaz had squeezed my ass to test for firmness and then had taken me to his room to bend me over his bed. That was the first time I'd been fucked, and sadly I now knew that the time you lose your virginity is supposed to be the time it feels worst. Even then, it felt so damn good that I couldn't stop from shooting. Now every time a top gets inside me, I love it so much I often come more than once.

Since that first night, the rest of my pledge class had advanced, and now even they got to fuck me if they wanted to. Dozens of guys had had my hole over the last four years, and I couldn't get enough. Jeez! What the hell was wrong with me?

I thought now about what Chaz had planned for today. I imagined he would have to do something different. Would I be able to keep from coming? I'd jerked off four times in the last twenty-four hours to make sure I could contain myself, each orgasm more violent than the last.

"And finally we come to secret societies," said Professor Whit, as he rose from his desk. "Do we have any members of the Laius League in the room? Perhaps a Chrysippus?"

My stomach lurched. Had he actually asked that? I shook it off. No reason to fear. It was a secret society. I wasn't supposed to reveal anything in public.

Then he raised his right hand, and I almost fell off my chair in shock. He was wearing a gold Laius ring.

"By rights, any Chrysippus in the room must reveal himself," the professor said in his rumbling Tennessee twang. He put his hands on his hips. "Mark Sanderson Cramer, are you here?"

I felt my face warm with humiliation and my dick tingled, beginning to stretch. I had no choice but to stand up.

"There he is!" the professor's voice thundered. "Class, for those who don't know, the Laius League has been around for over a hundred years, and each member who has passed initiation is a "Laius" or a leader. A Chrysippus is usually a freshman, indicating a submissive follower—one who needs to be taught and put through trials. However, Mark Sanderson Cramer is already a senior and still has not passed the trial, isn't that right?"

I looked down, aware that my face was red with humiliation. "No, sir. I have not passed."

The professor looked around the room and waved at me. "Look at him. Hollister shirt, penny loafers. Blond hair. He could be the preppie mascot of any school, but he is actually a secret slave." He snapped his fingers at me. "Strip, young man, because here is your final opportunity to pass the trial."

"What? Here? But I thought—?" I caught myself before I mentioned Chaz's name. Obviously Chaz had lied to me to keep me in the dark about the true nature of my final trial.

"Yes, Mr. Cramer. Here."

The students gave each other shocked looks and murmured. A couple of guys shook their heads and got up to leave.

"Don't anyone dare move!" shouted Professor Whit. The students sat back down.

I pulled my pants down, my stiffening dick getting tangled in my underwear. As I released it, my hard-on slapped against my stomach. My embarrassment made me so lightheaded I thought I might pass out. Timberlands was a small school. I had friends in that class whom I'd known for all four years, and now they were seeing my secret life.

"Class, Mark's trial and the trial of all Chrysippi is to get fucked in the ass and not come." There was a chorus of gasps and "holy shits."

"That trial should be simple enough, shouldn't it?" Professor Whit said, giving me a look that smoldered with lust. "Do you see how Mr. Cramer is now nude before us? This is only the beginning of the power of secret societies. This is how much Mr. Cramer desires to belong. Isn't that right?"

My breathing was hard, and I covered my penis with my hand, still dizzy with shame and excitement.

"Now he will lie down on his back on my desk, lift his legs in the air and offer his ass to get fucked in front of all of you."

"Please, sir," I stammered. "I...can't."

"You have no choice."

I whimpered and got on the desk. I'd expected at least some of the students to shake off their shock and walk out in disgust, but no one dared budge. Professor Whit opened the door to the class, and in came three students, all of them wearing masks over their eyes. Even with the masks, they looked vaguely familiar.

"These are the three most recent Laius League members to graduate to Laius status, and they are going to fuck Mark first, in front of all of you. They are freshmen. And isn't it the deepest humiliation for a senior to be gang fucked by freshmen?"

"Yes, sir," I responded. Since that first party where Chaz had chosen me, I'd secretly desired to be fucked in front of a room full of people, but I had never imagined anything like this. I shook my head. Why was I so hard? I needed to not want this. I needed to be a Laius and have all the advantages—easy admission to law school, guaranteed internships with members of congress, access to free first-class flights and executive positions at Fortune 500 companies. I had to try to focus on those positives while the first freshman, one of the few African-American students on campus, lifted my legs and lubed me up.

I could barely keep myself from hyperventilating as he lowered his pants, his thick erection bouncing. He was about to put on a condom when Professor Whit stopped him. "Terrence, in League gang bangs, we go in dick order to stretch out the bottom in increments. Colin, I believe you should begin."

Was he using their real names? I doubted it.

A scrawny boy who looked like he should still be in high school lowered his shorts and rubbed his dick against my buttcheeks to get it hard. I felt my face flaming at the unfairness that someone so young had the right to fuck my ass, and there was nothing I could do about it. Worse, I wanted his dick in me so bad, I nearly moaned. Colin may not have been as big as Terrence, but he was not small by any means.

In a flash, Colin had put a condom on and was pushing into my ass. I cried out as he pierced my sphincter, and everyone in the room gasped. I looked out at the class helplessly to see if they had turned their heads away, but they all were watching me get fucked. Seeing them staring at me sent a new burst of wonderful humiliation surging through my core.

"Just so you know, Mr. Cramer. You are the first Chrysippus to be fucked in public. Ever. Your inability to control your orgasm has led you to this predicament. Think about that."

My dick got harder. Why did he have to tell me that I was the only one to get ass-fucked in front of a class? Was I the only Chrysippus who never turned top? Was it possible that my ass was the most fucked in the history of Timberlands University? *God, how was I going to keep from coming now that I knew that?*

Colin savaged my hole for a full five minutes, and I moaned as he stretched me, but I took it like a man. I might have been put on display for the sake of shaming me, but I had pride in my ability to take dick. Against my will, my horniness overtook my embarrassment. If I could only hold on to the shame, I might have a chance at not coming. But I began to meet Colin's thrusts, and the rate of his respiration sped and his pumping got rougher. I felt the tightness of pleasure from my gut to my mouth. Just as I was getting close to the no-return point of orgasm, Colin came with a loud bark, to my great relief. He looked me in the eye with an expression of conquest and grinned a mean grin.

"Terrence, now you."

Even after I'd been nailed by Colin, Terrence was big enough that he had trouble stuffing himself in. He flipped me on all fours and began dicking me doggy-style. Now a few class members were taking pictures with their phones, probably sending them to everyone on campus.

"Mark's pussy is being taken bitch-style now," said Professor Whit, "and there's nothing he can do about it."

I winced at the burst of lust sparked by the professor's words. *Please don't let me come.*

The words also had an effect on Terrence.

"Yeah, Mark. Nothing you can do. Your ass is mine. All mine."

He kept repeating that. *Mine to fuck. Mine. All mine.*

If he kept fucking me much longer, I'd come. I knew what I

had to do even if it humiliated me beyond belief to say this to a freshman.

"Yes, sir," I said. "My ass is yours to fuck." The words made me feel the burn of sexual defeat. I'd been conquered for all to see, by a freshman no less.

Terrence growled and started nailing me with fury. Each stab in my hole shot heat up my spine to my brain. In mere moments, he brought himself to his peak and rammed in so deep that my neck jerked up with the jolt, and I nearly fell off the desk. There was some chuckling from the class, but I managed to take everything I was given, and I managed not to come.

"Thomas, your turn."

The third freshman, a lanky redhead, dropped his pants and sheathed his cock in latex. As he yanked my ass back with a nasty grip, I realized with horror that I knew him. Just last week, I'd had two Laius tops demand my ass at the same time, and I had to give it up to the more senior member. Thomas had to get to class and couldn't wait for his turn. He'd been incensed. As he slammed his huge dick into my rectum, I knew he was out for vengeance.

God, please don't make me come.

Thomas's dick found my prostate with every stroke, and I moaned in both euphoria and exquisite pain. My body rocked forward with each push. I couldn't believe I was taking such punishment. And I could do better. I arched up my rump to invite Thomas in deeper.

"Ah, yeah, boy. That's it," Thomas said. "Terrence, his ass is mine, not yours."

"Mark's ass belongs to all of you," said Professor Whit. "It belongs to everyone."

A fresh wave of heat consumed me. My dick throbbed. *Please, please don't come.*

"Cheer me on!" Thomas shouted at the class.

Terrence and Colin started chanting, "Fuck! That! Hole! Fuck! That! Hole!" until Thomas started ramming so hard that my grunts became shouts, and they had to yell louder to be heard over my voice.

Mercifully, I felt Thomas's condom flood as he collapsed on my back with a huge groan.

My eyes widened.

"I did it!" I exclaimed. "I didn't come."

Then I noticed Professor Whit had his pants down, exposing his truly massive erection.

"You're not done yet, Mr. Cramer. Flip over and put your legs back in the air."

I whimpered a protest, but in my mouth and my gut I felt a pulling, pulsing need to have the older man deep inside me. I got on my back. Terrence and Thomas each grabbed one of my ankles and spread my legs as wide as they could, making my hole as vulnerable as possible to penetration. Professor Whit lined up his enormous prick with my pucker. I cried out as he pushed in all the way to his balls.

I don't think I'd ever taken such a big penis before, and the burning and stretching was fantastic. I'd never felt more excited, nor more conquered and owned.

"With his legs in the air, he is most helpless. And not only do I have complete control over his ass, I also control his dick!"

No!

He grabbed my shaft and began pumping it. Every thrust sent a torrid wave of bliss from my hole to my entire body. I felt my balls rise, and I writhed, losing myself in the pleasure of his dick and hands.

"No, please!" I begged.

"Admit it, Mark. You're beaten. You're not Laius League

material because you love being submissive. Subs can't be men of power. You can't rule the world because your ass is conquered. The only thing you're good for is getting fucked!"

The combination of his humiliating words, his dick plundering my ass, and his hand pumping my cock was too much. I came and I came hard, all over my chest, neck and even my face.

"That's it! You've lost!" shouted Professor Whit. "And such a good ass. You're going to make me come, too."

The professor yanked my ass off the desk so he could impale me even deeper, and he roared as he filled his condom with semen.

"Class dismissed," said Professor Whit, panting. "Explaining the grip of secret societies as a force in alterity, as shown through the psychology of Mr. Cramer's submission, will be on the final."

The other students shuffled out, murmuring to each other in shock. My breath remained rapid, and the adrenaline from my orgasm still coursed through me.

"What do I do now?" I asked, wiping come from my cheek.

"You can't graduate. The League won't permit it."

"That's not fair! I passed all my classes."

"Too bad. As you might imagine, the League has influence with the board of trustees."

"I can't believe the school would let you get away with fucking me publicly! People outside the school...hell, people *everywhere* will hear about it!"

"This is my last year teaching, young man, and this was my last class. I've already quit, so they can't fire me. I'm independently wealthy and retiring young."

"But what about me? My future is...is ruined, isn't it?"

"You have two options. You could sue me and the school

for the humiliation and sexual misconduct, and you'll probably wind up with a few million dollars or"—here Professor Whit began to probe my hole with his fingers—"you can fulfill your destiny as my personal fuck slave who spends his life giving up his ass to me and all my friends."

I began to pant. "Oh, god," I said, imagining Professor Whit's huge and powerful dick inside me every day and being helpless to ever stop him.

"Somehow I think I know what you'll choose."

He lifted my legs and began to lube me up once more. I moaned and accepted my fate.

FRAT HOUSE MIDNIGHT SNACK

Jeff Funk

I'm standing in the laundry room of the frat with the lights off because I don't want any of the guys to see what I'm secretly up to, which happens to be sniffing Jason Orwell's jockstrap. Deeply I inhale—*balls*. My nostrils swoon from the manly musk, which strangely reminds me of hot plastic bubble wrap. There's sweat trapped in the still-moist mesh fabric, too; bitter like ammonia.

I reach again into his laundry bag, diving a hand farther, this time hoping to retrieve a sock. The smell of crotches, pits and feet makes me horny: man-stink. If given a chance, I'd like to lick each one of these spots on a dude—special attention on a dick. Damn, I'm dying to know what a cock feels like in my mouth. Mine's hot in my hands when I'm real turned on and jerking off to Internet porn. I switch the sucker in my mouth from my left cheek to my right. I like the suckers with gum or chewy stuff in the middle. Lately I've been into sucking on things because I so want a dick in between my lips, which are presently tinged cherry red, my favorite flavor. Boy, do I ever get the spit worked up. A guy's cock sliding in and out of my mouth? I'll bet that'd feel hot for him and me both.

There, found one: a nasty sweaty sock. I bring it to my nose. Damn, that's stinky. What the hell's going on between Jason's toes? Maybe I don't want to lick them after all. But I'll take another sniff. *Fuck, those are some dirty feet, Jason. Dirty boy. I'd like to have your feet on my crotch, stepping on it a little. Me lying on the floor, helpless beneath your jock foot. Maybe you'll crush my balls, squish them flat.* Man, that's totally sick. I notice, however, that my dick is hard as hell. I tug the waistband of my flannel leisure pants down and free my dick, a bouncy boner with an upward nature about it. Next I press myself against the cold side of the washing machine. Feels good. I close my eyes and begin to grind my hips, imagining rubbing my meat on Jason's hairy muscular body and possibly sticking it inside him.

Suddenly, I hear bare footsteps padding loudly down the stairs.

Whoa, shit, who's coming?

I duck down and spot a naked Kyle Warner loping down the stairs in front of the laundry room. It's a strange sight watching this athlete's body manage the last steps, nude and in mid-jig as if dancing a lopsided Irish dance. His dick swings long loops, flopping like a wild pendulum of flesh with some *weight* to it. The guy's carrying a monster between his legs.

A frequent naked wanderer of the halls, Kyle often stops by open doors to have a casual chat while on his way downstairs to fetch a snack from the kitchen. The rest of us are modest.

Now, I'm relieved he has no interest in coming into the laundry room. Instead, he struts sharply to the left toward the kitchen area of the house. I blow out a hot breath. *Whew. I don't*

*think he knows I'm in here. What's he up to? Going to raid the
fridge? The guy's always hungry.* I catch myself worrying again
that he knows I'm down here. *He didn't see me, right?* I wait
for a silent count of five and then tiptoe to the doorway to risk
a peek.

I see Kyle's naked ass jiggling. He has a cocky air about him
as he strides toward the kitchen, but then he turns left and goes
to the less-used side door.

I hear the sibilance of whispers, then see a masculine dad
type of guy with a mustache. He's in his thirties or older, forty
maybe. There's silver feathered among the dark hair over his
ears. He's wearing a black shiny winter coat, a red plaid scarf,
faded blue jeans and heavy boots like a construction worker's,
although he gives off the slick professional look of a white-
collar guy. He's built like Kyle—buff. He blows on his hands to
warm them from the cold and then he grabs Kyle's ass, a cheek
for each hand. Kyle leans in and kisses him.

I gasp in surprise. *He's gay.* I thought that I was the only one
in the house with a secret and secret crushes.

They look hot together, especially the contrast of the stranger
in clothes and Kyle being buck naked. They kiss with tongues.
Kyle's hands probe inside the stranger's coat in search of bare flesh
like his own. Then they hold hands and walk into the kitchen.

Silence.

I realize my dick's painfully straining to unfold from its
own taut sheath of skin. It's trapped. I adjust and pull it so I'm
packing to the left of my underwear inside my flannels.

Maybe I'm hungry, I suddenly think. I could fake being
surprised by the sight of them and then promise not to tell on
him. I like knowing other people's secrets. I smile at the notion
of being able to call in a favor. I decide to go to the kitchen—I'm
hungry, after all.

My first steps are soft and tentative. Soon I pick up a strut, even though my insides feel like they're fluttering away from me. I'm filled with a sexual charge that makes me shake.

When I arrive in the doorway, I'm surprised to find that the kitchen is empty. My eyes blink over toward the closed door that leads to the basement. They must be down there.

Rodney's music from upstairs sounds bass heavy here in the kitchen. I hear muffled thumps. Rod has his girlfriend in his room, banging her. It's a nightly thing. He cranks the tunes to cover up the sound of her baby-doll, high-pitched squeals. The last girlfriend he had was pretty quiet, sort of a dead lay—letting out a few moans, at most.

In the basement are storage lockers for personal belongings. There's also a back section that's crammed full of the makings for the float we use in the parade at the end of Greek Week. Other than that, the only things down there are the ice machine and a half-bath—a dirty toilet that nobody uses, except for Tommy Mandinelli who likes to take a solitary crap in the afternoons. He probably jerks off in there, too.

I'll bet that's where they went.

Opting for a quick change of plans, I open a cupboard, select the ice bucket and cradle it under my left armpit. Then I take a couple of stealthy steps next to the fridge and reach for the basement door with my right hand. The brass knob has a smooth surface, which reflects my trembling fingers, making them look chubbier than they really are.

The door swings open with ease, and after taking two steps down, I close it behind me. My bare feet move tentatively as I skulk down the stairs with toes splayed, anticipating each lower level. When I'm almost to the bottom, a board beneath me creaks with a groan like an old man belching. Rodney's music is barely audible now. Instead I hear deep male moans that are somewhat timed with the beats coming from the faint speakers.

They are *in the toilet.* I walk over to the door and put my ear to it. "Uh, uh, uh," grunts a bass voice. The sound thrills me. *Is Kyle fucking that guy's ass? Or is he getting fucked? Who's doing what to whom? Wish I could see in there!*

That crapper is fucking disgusting. It has a sink, a toilet and ancient puke caked in a couple spots on the floor that nobody ever bothers to clean up. *Fuck, I ain't doing it.*

I listen a while longer then I walk behind a storage locker and peer between two boxes. While I'm hidden deep in the shadows, the door to the toilet has me transfixed. I'm filled with longing to be inside there along with those two studs, feasting on their Greek god-like bodies. I breathe shallow breaths, pull my pants down and begin jerking off. As their groans escalate, I can't hold back any longer. I cup my hand around the head of my dick and blast shot after shot of jism into my palm. Since I don't have anything to wipe it on, I make a split-second decision to force it into my mouth and swallow it before it cools. I hate eating cold cum—my own, anyway. Like coffee, it has to be hot for me to like it. In fact, usually after I've shot, the urge to lick up my mess leaves me fast; I have to make myself do it. *Wonder how it would be, eating another guy's jizz?*

Abruptly, the door clicks open.

"Thanks, man," Kyle says. He buttons the stranger's coat for him and adjusts his scarf.

The guy gives a final tug on Kyle's dick, which is still beefed up, and kisses him deeply as if to thank him and say good-bye for the night. They go upstairs. I wait until I hear the floor creaking with their footsteps across the kitchen overhead, then I go to the toilet and walk inside.

Sex.

I can smell it. My dick is still plump.

* * *

The next day, the first thing I think of is Kyle and that guy doing it in the basement toilet. My dick's more swollen than usual—*petrified* morning wood. It aches in a good way as I jack myself with rabbit-quick short strokes, my other hand firmly squeezing my balls. *Where did he meet that guy, on the Internet? Probably. I've seen the sex listings.* I replay images from the night's dirty happenings and continue pleasuring myself.

Aw fuck, there we go. Yeah boy, shoot this all over Kyle's huge fuckin' dick.

I squirt a giant mess all over myself, my flat stomach receiving most of it. A few drops make it to my chest. I scoop up a droplet of cum dripping near my nipple and slide that finger into my mouth—yum, not too cold. The mildly fishy taste of my semen mixes with my morning breath. I smack my lips and feel like a dirty boy. I figure that since I like the taste of cum so much, maybe someday I'll become a connoisseur of other men's nut loads. I spring from my bed, open my closet door and reach for my robe and shower caddy 'cause, man, I gotta brush my teeth.

There's nobody in the hallway. I'm kind of glad since my cock is trying to part my robe, and I can't reach down and tend to it. I'm carrying my caddy in one hand and the other, with my key around the wrist, is closing the door.

I go about my morning rituals: brush my teeth, take a dump. The floor tile in the bathroom feels cold against my bare feet. There are two bathrooms on this floor, one at each end of the long hallway. As I'm in the shower soaping my pecker, I obsess over how I could get with Kyle. I start my mental dreams of how-it-might-gos and what-I-coulda-dones last night—the whole mix—and then I'm suddenly remembering something.

Kyle came on to me one night.

Holy shit. When it happened I thought for sure he was jerkin' my chain, acting a little queer just to make fun, but now I realize that the fucker is so good he passes for straight; he's that secure with himself. Neat trick. He hides in plain sight.

That night, we had one hell of a party going on and everyone was puking in the bushes. Kyle and I had slipped out to his LeSabre in the parking lot to smoke a joint. After about ten or fifteen minutes of passing it back and forth, we each had a strong buzz going on. That's when we saw Sean pull up in his Bronco, and immediately after he got out, he started undoing his fly to relieve himself. It was around eleven-thirty—I know because that's when the late night train passes by the fence just beyond the frat parking lot—and I'll never forget this. Kyle was about to get out of the car to go back to the frat, but when he saw the guy fishing his cock out of his pants, he said, "Oh, wait. I want to see Sean's dick."

As the night train went by, we watched Sean take a long piss, shake his flaccid member, and then zip up. I tell ya, the scene seemed to last *forever* under the time-warp influence of marijuana, playing like an epic movie washing over us, so vivid and erotic. My hearing was distorted, with everything—the rumbling of the locomotive's wheels, the blare of its powerful whistle—sounding like it was being piped through a distant running fan. Neither of us said a word while watching the stream of piss arching from Sean's penis, splattering the blacktop of the parking lot. I've always wondered if Kyle's eerie silence and the subtle way he parted his legs was an invitation or a test. *Maybe*, I thought then, *he's fucking with me to see what I'll do, but it's probably a pot thing. He's stoned*. Like usual, I froze; I did nothing.

Now, here in the shower, with my hand pounding my meat for the second time already today, I understand that it was a missed opportunity to suck his dick. Well, I'm not going to let that happen again. Hell, I need to take some fucking risks if I'm going to get what I want. Lord knows being a goody two-shoes wasn't getting a cock in my mouth. Time to be bold, I figure. Guys like blow jobs from guys. Tonight, when Kyle takes his evening shower around midnight, I'm going to try something…

Ah, there.

I bust a nut amidst the strong, blasting spray of the hot water in my shower. Cum clings to my fingers, especially between them, even though they're wet. You wouldn't think it would stick to skin so much. I lick my hand off, tasting my salty load and slightly metallic water—yum, hot like I like it.

Later that night, after spending most of the day fighting off boners—my dick having leaked numerous slimy strands, staining the inside of my boxer-briefs something terrible—I wait in a lounge chair in the common area that separates the rows of bedrooms upstairs.

Kyle's room is at the other end of the hall from mine, which means he uses that side's sinks, crappers and two shower stalls. It's the messy bathroom. Those idiots are always buzzing their hair and then leaving it in the sink and all over the floor. I see it when I walk by. They don't clean up after themselves at all. It's fitting that brazen, nudist Kyle goes to that set of showers along with the cruder guys. We're a prissy bunch at my end, the clean freaks.

So here I am, sucking on a cherry sucker with my leg sprawled over the arm of the club chair, looking chilled out. I'm texting with this girl in my physics class, a fellow night owl, as I wait for Kyle to come out of his room and head for the shower. When it gets to be around twenty minutes past midnight, my heart starts to sink because I'm thinking that maybe he has fallen asleep and gotten out of his routine, but then I hear his bedroom door pop open.

There he is.

That tight ass of his jiggles with each of his long-legged strides. He looks so fine with a towel draped over his shoulder, cocky stud. His door swings shut behind him with a loud slam. I close my phone and pocket it, then crawl from my chair to follow my prey.

I slow down when I get close to the last bedroom before the alcove leading to the bathroom, which has no door. Rather, the layout of the architecture gives privacy along with the ability to walk freely in there—a long cement wall, then a turn, and you're in the bathroom. The ceiling light is out above this section of the corridor. It's dark other than the red EXIT sign above the stairwell and the glow of the lights coming from the bathroom.

I hear a urinal flush although I didn't hear the sound of pissing first. Some guys do that—give the tank a flush so there's sound to get them started. *Maybe Kyle's pee shy*, I think. *How strange to be a nudist but timid about taking a piss.* Then I hear him going, a strong stream, and I find myself wondering what it would be like to hold on to his cock for him while it comes out. Next the shower starts up. I venture beyond the cement wall and peer inside, watching his reflection in a mirror. *Man, look at that bubble butt.* I watch while he waits for the water to get hot enough. It's not long before steam starts floating toward the mirrors, steaming them up and obstructing my view. The smeary reflection of his naked body disappears when he hops into the shower.

The setup of the men's room seems to have been made for modest men: a bank of three sinks, two crappers side by side, and an east private shower and one to the west. There are floor-to-ceiling shower curtains for them both. The one where Kyle is presently showering is next to the heavily frosted window to the outside. It's farthest from the doorway and more private than the one that faces the two crappers. Most men choose the window shower because sometimes guys will stank you out, which is *bad* when there's steam from a shower involved. The stink, jeez.

I go to the toilet that's next to the wall. I undo my pants, letting them fall, and then sit down as if to use it, but really I'm getting myself naked gradually and still working up my nerve. *Am I going to do this? Fuck, yes. Go for it, just suck his dick.* I kick off my shoes and step out of my jeans and boxer-briefs, leaving them bunched up on floor. Then I hoist my shirt over my head and toss it onto my pile of clothes. I'm completely naked aside from my Om necklace.

Rodney's music is playing from his room down the hall. As usual, he's in there putting it to Baby Doll. Shit, I've learned to tune her out. Here in the bathroom, I can hear Kyle humming along to the song. Suddenly, he honks his nose into his hands. It's a hell of a noise that echoes loudly through the bathroom.

Crude.

Barefoot, I pad closer to his side, passing the bank of sinks. The bulb over the middle basin is flickering. I toss my sucker into the plastic lining of the wastebasket. As I approach the frosted window to the cold outdoors, I turn to the left.

I'm at his shower.

I stare at the bottom folds of the shower curtain and focus on a wet foot with matted dark tufts of hair fanned across the toes. *Be bold,* I tell myself. Then I reach for the curtain and part it.

Kyle's eyes are closed while the back of his head is being sprayed by the force of the water. He reaches for the soap dispenser to get some of the combination body wash and shampoo gel. He opens his eyes and then jumps back, startled by my presence. "Jesus, what the—?" he starts to say, but when he sees that my gaze goes down to his dick, he understands that he's about to get a blow job. His eyes are filled with an animal emotion, alluring yet dangerous. He now steps to widen the distance between his feet, further exposing his penis, which is dripping with a stream of water that gives him the illusion of pissing like a fountain. His body language tells me to come in, so I step into the stall and close the curtain behind me.

The water is hot.

Kyle's dick starts swelling before I even wrap my shaky fingers around its girth and continues growing as I hold it. The shaft has a thick vein running down the middle. I jack him slowly, learning what it feels like to play with a penis other than my own. I cup his balls with reverence, then squat down and press my lips to his dick and kiss his piss slit.

I taste him, running my tongue in swirls and milking the sensitive skin gathered beneath the rim of his cockhead with my lips. It's slippery in my mouth and warm. Heat emanates from his manhood, and it's mixed with the temperature of the water. I test how much of it I can take before it makes me gag. I feel tears come to my eyes the first time I sputter on it, but keep coming back for more. I think, *Now I've gone and done it. I'm a dirty boy. I'm gonna be a cock-hungry slut boy from here on.*

"Oh, that's good," Kyle says in a breathy whisper. "Could you, like, take it *all* the way again? That feels fuckin' hot, dude."

"Sure."

He then grabs hold of my wet, thick hair and forces my face to take his cock until my nose mashes into his pubes. I surprise myself, swallowing five of his face-fucking thrusts before I choke his cock back out, leaving a long strand of saliva drizzling from his peter down to my left knee. I admire the way the water pastes the dark hair on his legs to his skin. He grabs my head and fucks my face again. It only takes a few slips into my esophagus to make him start squirting. As soon as I taste his jizz and feel the throbbing of his cock, I work my lips to make it feel even better for him. He tastes so good. I use my tongue on the head, teasing his pisshole, but this makes him jump back. "Ah, sensitive," he says.

"Sorry." I stand up next to him and look at his handsome face.

He takes my boner into his strong, frat boy hand and jerks me rapidly. I'm panting with my eyes closed when I feel his tongue ramming into my mouth. He pumps my meat until he makes me shoot—cum flies onto the shower curtain, out to the tile floor and swirling down the drain. We kiss, embracing as hot water sloshes our bodies. My hug slides down the skin of his back until I'm caressing the firm halves of his butt. I close my eyes and kiss his neck. Finally, he turns off the water.

As he towels off, he blows a quick breath. "Whew," he says, and then hands me his used towel so I can dry myself. He seems sweet. In that moment of connection, my heart skips in my chest from the glimmer of brotherly tenderness between men. Then he takes his towel back from me, slings it over his shoulder and strolls away, probably off to the kitchen for a snack. I go to the toilet stall and step back into my clothes, pulling them onto my damp body. Face blushing, I'm feeling dirty but also savoring my first taste of another man's cum. A coating of it sticks pleasantly in the back of my throat, a residue for me to remember that I had Kyle's dick deep inside, and he got off from my mouth. Got off *in* my mouth—*cum,* hot like I like it.

CREAMED

Landon Dixon

began to question the whole point of belonging to a fraternity when I was instructed to jerk off into the dean's morning cup of coffee as part of my initiation.

Emilio Rodriguez took me aside and explained it to me. "The dean's secretary always brings him a fresh cup of coffee first thing in the morning. All you have to do is hang around outside the dean's office while I phone in a distraction, and then slip right on inside and jack off into his coffee. Nothing to it."

The tall, thin, creamed-coffee-colored frat brother threw an arm around my shoulder and grinned down at me, full of confidence—that I was going to be caught and expelled, no doubt. "Uh, can't I just kidnap Benny the Beaver and let him loose in the zoology department's boreal forest exhibit?" I asked. Benny the Beaver was the mascot for the school's football team, the Snapping Beavers.

"No dice, pledge," Emilio replied happily, squeezing my shoulder encouragingly. "You do this and you won't have to do anything else during pledge week. Not a bad deal, huh?"

"Couldn't I just spit in the dean's coffee?" I persisted. Even with my hair-trigger hand and cock, jerking off was going to take some time, leaving me exposed in more ways than one.

Emilio's arm slipped off my shoulder, the good-looking guy's brown eyes going from soft to hard. "You bucking a frat brother's command, pledge?"

My shoulders slumped without the support. "No," I groaned.

The dean's office was located in the two-hundred-year-old administrative building that had formerly housed the entire college, before expansion. He was up on the third floor; his office opened up at 8:30 A.M. I was outside in the hall at eight, wearing a pair of sweatpants and no underwear for quick and easy access and a guilty as hell expression on my freckled face.

A man came trotting down the hall toward the dean's door, and I turned and scrupulously studied the painting of the first dean, Rev. Harding Manners, on the wall opposite. From the corner of my nervous gray eyes, I saw the man pull a key out of his pocket, stick it in the lock and open the door.

He went inside, shutting the door behind him. I glanced up and down the empty hallway, my dick as scared as the rest of me, then pushed the door open and went on through.

The dean's outer office was small and formal, carpeted in blood red, dark wood paneling on the walls. There were three hard-backed wooden chairs, and a desk where the man with the key was standing. He was darker than the wood, mahogany in color, short and slim and fine-featured, with brown eyes and black hair, dressed in a pair of dark-blue slacks, a white dress shirt and a blue blazer. He sort of looked like Carlton from "The Fresh Prince of Bel-Air," only thinner and less obnoxious.

"Can I help you?" he asked.

His voice was as cultivated as his manner. "Um, yeah, I wanted to see the dean."

He gave me the once-over. My sweatpants and T-shirt seemed woefully out of place, like the whole crazy scheme. "Do you have an appointment?"

"N-no!" I gulped.

"Well, you have to have an appointment. The dean's a very busy man, you know."

"Oh, okay!" I turned and wrestled with the polished brass doorknob, which kept slipping out of my sweaty hand. There were plenty of other fraternities on campus. Hazing seemed like a welcome prospect.

"If it's really important, the dean *might* be able to see you right at 8:30, first thing when he comes in."

I barely heard the guy. Why the hell didn't he just let me flee? "Oh, okay," I mouthed, staring at the heavy, dark wood of the door.

"You can sit down and wait, if you like," Andrew said after a minute or so.

That was his name—Andrew Cole. I got that from his brass nameplate when I finally got my muscles working again and turned around. I limped over to a chair and sat down. Andrew smiled coolly at me. I blushed back, as I told him my name was Rufus Nerdlinger. I didn't think well under pressure.

The minutes dragged by like a public affairs lecture, my brief college career flashing before my eyes. Was coming in someone's coffee vandalism, assault or an act of terrorism? Why the hell hadn't I taken Viagra or something, arrived with an already loaded pair of pants?

The hands on the grandfather clock in the corner trembled arthritically around to 8:30, and at that exact instant, the outer door burst open and the dean of the university stormed in. I just about jumped up out of my chair and through the window behind Andrew.

"Good morning, Dean Skinner," the cool and composed assistant said to his boss.

"Morning, Andrew!" the dean boomed—and then stopped and stared at me. "And what do we have here?"

If I could've crawled into a knothole in the wood paneling and pulled it in after me, I would've. The dean was big and white haired, not a man to mess with. My face blushed red.

"This young man is Rufus Nerdlinger. He needs to see you, Dean. Apparently, quite urgently."

"Well, okay! I've got a few minutes before my first appointment," the dean said, glancing at his watch. "Come into my office." He turned to Andrew. "Bring my coffee in, too, will you?"

Coffee. My loins shriveled at the very word.

The man's office was lined with books and paintings and furnished with leather chairs and a huge walnut desk as old and distinguished as the college itself. Andrew brought in a cup in a saucer and set it down on the dean's desk, as the man himself settled down into his high-backed, padded chair. The coffee was black and steaming.

Andrew was just about to leave the two of us alone, when the dean suddenly raised a hand and yelled, "Wait a minute, Andrew, you forgot my cream!"

I shriveled another few inches.

"Sorry, my mistake. I'll get it for you."

A phone rang in the outer office.

"Sit down."

"Can I see you for a moment, Dean," Andrew suddenly interjected, sticking his head back into the open door.

The dean got up from his desk and exited the office.

The phone call, the cup of coffee on the desk. It was all coming together.

I heard muffled voices outside, as I slipped over to the dean's desk and stood in front of his cup of coffee. I looked down at it. I picked up the cup and turned toward the door. I pulled my cock out of my pants and started stroking.

I wasn't thinking, just doing, the key to any half-cocked stunt. I wasn't anywhere near erection, let alone ejaculation. A door slammed. I frantically tugged on my cock, which, due to nerves, I couldn't get hard.

"What are you doing?"

I almost jumped out of my skin. My cock leapt right into the steaming hot coffee. "Yow!" I howled.

Andrew rushed around the desk and stared at me as I held the coffee cup in one hand and my cock in the other. I was suspended in time, motion and fear.

But then a smile broke over Andrew's plush lips, and his eyes beamed warmly. He walked closer to me, took my cock out of my hand and bent down and kissed it. "There, does that feel better?"

I gaped at the guy. My cock surged with blood—in Andrew's warm, soft palm. He pulled gently on it, making me shiver with disbelief and excitement.

"The dean won't be back for a while," he stated, relieving me of the coffee cup and setting it back down on the desk. He stroked me hard and long, my body and dick flooding with dizzying heat.

He kissed me on the mouth. His lips were soft and wet. I sighed, blissfully. Things had changed so suddenly, my emotions roller-coasting from fear to lust. Andrew fondled my cock and kissed me. He dropped down on his knees, and took the swollen tip of my cock into his mouth.

"Oh, yes!" I moaned.

Andrew's lips enveloped my purple knob. He consumed my prick in a liquid heat even more wicked than the coffee, fondling my balls with his agile fingers.

I sunk my hands into his hair, urging him on. It was like the room was spinning. I'd come to play a pledge prank, and here I was getting my cock played by a virtuoso.

Andrew dove his mouth down to his hand and back up on my cock. "Jesus!" I cried. "I'm gonna come!"

He picked the coffee cup up off the desk and pointed my pipe at the dark contents. "Come in this," he said. "I just ate breakfast and there's nothing else handy."

Practical, as well as sexual; the man was damn near perfect.

Orgasm tidal-waved through my spasming body, up from my balls and on through my shaft.

I bucked, blasting semen into the coffee. Andrew had a heck of a time keeping me down and on target, but he obviously had a master's degree, the way he mastered my dick. He didn't spill a drop, aiming my entire load into the cup, creaming the coffee but good.

"Your turn," he said at the spluttering end, unhanding me and climbing to his feet.

I thought about the dean storming back in at any moment. I thought about...then I saw Andrew's dong, as he pulled it out of his dress pants. And I thought about nothing more than loving that ebony appendage.

His cock was long and thick and as black as coffee, a single swollen vein running down the shining top. I dropped to my knees in awe and grasped it in my worshipping hands.

He grunted and jerked. I stroked with both hands, covering every velvety inch of his dick with my covetous palms. I fisted, pumping up from his balls to his cap, shunting slick foreskin back and forth.

I dropped one hand off and cupped his hanging balls, squeezed the heavy, dangling sac. He groaned and grabbed at my hair, thrusting his cock into my moving hand. I jacked his cock and juggled his balls, staring into the stunning darkness of his powerful loins.

"Suck me!" he gasped.

I licked my lips and looked at his beefy, purple-black cap. Then I opened my mouth and popped the hood inside, mouthing his knob like he'd mouthed mine. He reacted the same way, moaning and sinking his fingernails into my scalp.

I sealed my lips tight to his hood and tugged, twisting his balls with my hand. His body bent and his mouth gaped, my own maw full of that chew-toy top of his cock. I had to have more, all if I could manage it. I opened my mouth and throat as wide as they'd go and swallowed up his cock inch by hard inch.

I couldn't consume his entire snake, just more than enough for both of us. I kept him locked down and shivering like that for a while, then pulled my head back and pushed it forward.

"Yes, that's it!" he hissed, pumping to meet my sucking.

He jerked my head. My mouth slid up and down his incredible length. I gagged a few times, but I kept on.

"Get the cup! Get the cup!"

I blinked my eyes open, tears streaking down my cheeks. I grabbed the coffee cup off the desk, and Andrew yanked his dong out of my mouth, leaving me achingly empty. I filled the void by grabbing onto his dripping cock and pumping hard and quick, aiming that mammoth hood at the brew I'd already seasoned with my own creamer.

Andrew jerked and jetted, his cock going off with a spurt in my jacking hand. He splattered a rope of white-hot jizz into the coffee, then another, and another, and another, his pressurized hose jumping in my hand. I had a heck of a time controlling it.

Just as I pumped the last drop of cream out of his slit, the outer door suddenly opened and closed.

"Get up! Quick!" Andrew rasped, pulling his spent snake out of my hand and tucking it into his pants, gesturing at me with his free hand.

I jumped to my feet, jostling the heady brew in its cup.

"There was no emergency down in the women's dorm shower room, Andrew!" Dean Skinner blustered, barreling into his office. "Someone must've got their wires crossed."

He looked at me. "Ah, my coffee! Properly creamed now, I see."

He reached forward to take the cup from me. And I did the only thing I could think of to maintain my academic standing— I drank down the frothy beverage in three hearty gulps.

The dean stared at me. Andrew grinned at me.

I found out the true nature of the prank—played on me—later that day when I saw Dean Skinner's handsome secretary and Brother Emilio making out like madmen behind the library building. They'd obviously been in cahoots on the whole thing, Andrew giving and getting a good blow job while Emilio got a good laugh.

I wasn't too disappointed, though. Despite the fact that my reckless actions counted for nothing in my quest to be fully pledged, hadn't the pair shown me what true Greek fraternity between men was all about?

STRIPPED

Rachel Kramer Bussel

When the doorbell rang, Donnie was tasked with answering it. He was the low man on the totem pole in their frat house, and he'd been the one ordered to call for a stripper. Little did he know that his higher-ups had given him the number of a very special strip club, and when Cherry arrived, she had quite the surprise for him—and the rest of the group. Cherry was one of the most fabulous women Donnie had ever seen, with lips plumped to perfection, black curls falling perfectly down her shoulders, skin so bronzed he couldn't tell if it was natural or tanner, and tits that bulged almost unnaturally. When Cherry said hello, though, that's when Donnie got a sinking feeling in his stomach, though his boner stayed in place. Cherry was a guy, or at least, had been, once.

"Hey, baby, I'm ready for a good time," Cherry said, her lipstick matching her name, her elongated eyelashes sparkling.

"Um, just a second, you can wait right here," Donnie said, his eyes wide, his mind whirring as he tried to process what had just happened. Jason had been adamant that Donnie use that number, not just find an ad in the back of the local alt weekly, and whatever Jason said, went, at least, as far as Donnie was concerned. The house had a definite pecking order and while there were a few guys with more power than Jason, there were none who deigned to talk to Donnie.

He found Jason smoking a joint and laughing uproariously at something one of their fellow frat brothers had just said. "Um, Jason, I need to talk to you," Donnie said, pushing his glasses up on his nose. For the umpteenth time, he wondered what exactly had compelled him to pledge a frat; his best friend, Margot, had been encouraging him to get out there and make new friends; she'd insisted it would look good to future employers and would show him to be "one of the boys." But he had quickly sensed that he was not exactly one of the boys—and not just because late at night he had fantasies and dirty dreams, wet dreams, perverse dreams—about some of the boys he shared a home with, not to mention professors, celebrities and strangers. He wasn't into the whole getting wasted, being loud, being wild and crazy thing which most of the brothers were. A few were more serious and studious, interested in the world around them rather than just their highly specific surroundings, and when he could indulge in a three-hour conversation about history or an article in the paper or even their future, he was happy.

"What's the matter, Donnie-boy?" Jason laughed in his face.

"The stripper, Cherry, I think—"

"Then bring her in, the boys are ready for a show, aren't they?" Jason's look dared Donnie to protest, but he didn't.

He slunk back to Cherry, who was standing on five-inch heels looking every inch the divine creation she was. She was over-the-top in every sense of the word, and without her coat, he saw that she was poured into an outfit that looked to Donnie like a bathing suit but could've been a leotard; he didn't know about such things. He did know that his heart had started to pound, hard, when he approached Cherry, trying not to stare at her Adam's apple. "The boys are ready for you," Donnie said diplomatically, like he was ushering in a guest speaker, rather than a lap dancer.

"But are you ready for me, honey?" Cherry asked, giving Donnie a wink and bending down to kiss his cheek, smelling of powder and perfume, her breasts just touching Donnie. He couldn't answer the question, in part because Cherry had already started walking toward the living room and in part because he had no idea. Just what was going to happen when Cherry stripped down? Would the boys revolt? Would they hurt her? Would they hurt Donnie?

Donnie followed her and cleared his throat, then announced as loudly as he could, "Everyone, this is Cherry. She's here to entertain us."

The boys hooted and whistled, and then Donnie felt himself being hoisted up by a pair of strong, firm hands. "She definitely is, and so are you, Donnie!" Jason's voice boomed in his ear. He was trembling but again, his dick got hard; maybe, he thought, it liked the excitement that the fear of the unknown could bring.

"What do you mean?" Donnie asked.

"You're going to be rewarded for all the grunt work you've been doing for us." His eyes, from what Donnie could tell, gleamed, as he pushed Donnie into a chair and, moments later, secured his hands behind his back. "Cherry, we're ready for you," someone called, and soon the lights dimmed marginally, and suddenly Cherry's breasts and sweet perfume (did he imagine it or did she smell like her name?) were right in his face.

"Hey, baby, don't worry about a thing, okay?" she whispered in Donnie's ear. It was a do-or-die moment; he knew if he wanted to, he could make a huge fuss, get them to untie him, and make his escape. But he stayed, and it wasn't just to tough it out and get through the hazing process. He stayed because of Cherry; because, even though he couldn't let the boys see it, he suddenly wanted to see just what she had to offer.

"Why don't you boys start the music?" Cherry didn't seem fazed at all by the obviously rowdy boys' club atmosphere; to Donnie, it just made her seem more self-possessed, like she was above all this; as if she were there not for the money but for the chance to teach the boys a thing or two. Maybe that was what Donnie wanted to learn from her—how to not let them get to him.

Soon a song he knew about from his older brother filled the room; "Pour Some Sugar on Me." It was Def Leppard, that much he knew, but he didn't care who sang it because there was Cherry, not just singing, but embodying the song. As his brothers drew back in awe and appreciation, Donnie had Cherry all to himself, and she reached into her bra and pulled out sugar packs, ripping them open in time to the music and coating her now-sweaty skin with the tiny granules. Cherry was whipping her hair around, whizzing her body right by his face, and there was nothing Donnie could do about the erection pressing upward against his pants, and part of him was glad. If his hands had been free, surely he'd have reached up for a taste of his own personal cherry pie.

But the dancer was ready to give that to him, without him having to move. Her eyes met Donnie's for a brief second, and an electric flash of desire raced through him. In a flash of insight, he realized that he liked her, he wanted her, and not just the girlie parts; he wanted what was between Cherry's legs. "I think Donnie has a woody," one of the guys called out and moments later, another had walked up and unzipped his pants, so that

Donnie, too, was stripping for them. The homoerotic implications of this seemed lost on the guys as they teased Donnie over the music.

"Cherry, do you want some cream in your pie?" one of them called out. She whipped around and moved toward the guy who'd spoken.

"What are you trying to ask me, sugar?" Her voice was syrupy sweet but Donnie thought he detected a slight edge just beneath it.

"Not me—him!" the boy who Donnie recognized as Adrien piped up.

"What, you don't have any cream in your cup for me?" she asked, reaching down to fondle his dick. Donnie's eyes widened as Adrien's cheeks turned red, though a part of him was suddenly jealous; why was Adrien getting her attention when he clearly didn't want it, while Donnie's dick was rock hard, a fact that everyone in the room could see?

Cherry soon returned to him and leaned down enough for his cock to brush against her breasts. "I'm not leaving you, sweetie," she said, patting his cheek. There was something at once disconcerting and sexy about her sweet, sexy, feminine voice and the cock Donnie knew was tucked between her legs. Suddenly he wanted to see it, hold it, taste it. He might not feel that way about cocks of any of the guys in the room, but hers, yes, hers he wanted.

Donnie opened his mouth to say something, but Cherry put her finger to his lips. Her skin on his was warm and made him forget, for a moment, about where they were; he just wanted more of her body against his. When the song switched to "Cherry Pie," the namesake dancer really went to town, even bending her body at the waist and swooping down so it seemed like she was taking a swipe at Donnie's cock. He moaned, not caring who saw; he'd be shocked if some of the other guys weren't aroused despite themselves. They'd hired a "she-male" stripper to have a laugh on him, but who was laughing now, as Cherry pulled her breasts out of her top and slapped them against Donnie's face?

He could still hear the music, but it had grown distant; it was as if Cherry were giving him a rebirth, a way out, a carnal knowledge worth far more than what she was being paid. It wasn't just his cock that had come alive, but all his senses, as she put so much more than shaking her booty into the song. When Cherry's cock brushed against Donnie's leg, he shivered. Cherry leaned down, her sweet smell wafting up his nose. "I think we should get out of here after my dance. Come let me show you a good time. On the house. You look like you don't belong here. Or maybe you do, but you could use some cock." Her words were spoken in that same sultry voice, one so feminine it would've been jarring if Donnie wasn't already under her spell.

But Cherry's words were anything but jarring; they were an erotic escape route, a way out from the torment he'd thought he had to suffer at the hands of these boys. He was a virgin, but that didn't mean Donnie hadn't thought about things, late at night. He'd seen boys in the locker room at school passing by clad only in towels, and he had wondered. He'd watched girls and guys making out and couldn't tell which one he wanted. Cherry was offering him a little of each, and he watched as she turned her back to him and took none other than Jason's hand and placed it on the hardness she was no longer trying to hide. He shut his eyes and mock-shuddered, but was that a stiffy pressing against Jason's pants, too? Was getting turned on by a guy okay as long as he didn't look like a guy?

Donnie didn't care anymore; he just watched, soaking her in as Cherry did complete justice to Warrant's epic anthem. No, she didn't pull a cherry pie out of her panties, but she did shake her ass enough to give some of Donnie's "brothers" whiplash.

When she finally leaned over him and planted a juicy kiss directly on his lips, she was dripping in sweat, but Donnie didn't mind. She stared deeply into his eyes, but only for a moment before the boys started to swarm in. Then Cherry did something that Donnie would never forget; she pulled a pen out of somewhere, and scrawled her number across his palm, then curled his fingers up, kissed him and left.

They untied him, then made him chug enough beer to satisfy them. He felt like he was just going through the motions until he could get away and dial her number.

He didn't get a chance to till the next day. When he did, the person who answered didn't sound like Cherry at all. "Who's this?" asked a man with a husky voice.

"Uh, this is Donnie. From last night...The, uh, party." He didn't want to give too much away in case it wasn't actually Cherry on the line.

"Oh, hey, sexy," the person said. "I'm Charles. Did you want to get together?" Charles named a gay bar in town.

"I, well, um...sure," Donnie mumbled, not actually sure at all, but he knew he couldn't refuse. He'd been given an opportunity to see how the other half lived, and he needed to pursue it.

Without telling anyone, he dressed in black, sneaking out at midnight, just as the house was settling down. He got to the bar, grateful that he had managed to avoid any of the other guys; after they'd seen him "humiliated," he'd gained a twisted kind of cred. "Hey, baby," said a familiar voice, coming from a pair of unfamiliar lips. These weren't painted anything but a natural, dusky pink.

Donnie's cock stirred, but this time he wasn't surprised. He hadn't just been thinking about Cherry's tits. "Hey," he said, his eyes briefly surveying the bar, willing himself not to feel out of place in his dorky glasses; why hadn't he gotten contacts yet?

"Did you come here to kiss me for real?" Charles asked; then, before Donnie could answer, the other man had pressed his lips right up against his. He'd had pretend kisses with girls in high school, two of them, but nothing like this. This was for real, and every cell in Donnie's body knew it. He opened his mouth and let Charles slide his tongue between his lips. Charles's fingers worked their way through Donnie's short hair.

"Who have we here?" Donnie heard from behind him, and he looked around to find a drag queen in full regalia, glittering in black sequins, with legs that went on forever.

"Just a frat boy I found," Charles said and laughed.

"A frat boy, eh?" the stranger said, surveying Donnie.

"He's a kid, leave him alone," Charles said, laying his hand protectively on Donnie's arm. They spent about an hour at the bar before Charles said, "Let's get out of here." Donnie could've refused, of course, but then he'd have been passing up the chance to figure out if what he was feeling was real, although his stiff cock could've told him perfectly well that it was.

He was fascinated by Charles/Cherry: his dual life, his sexy voice, his sheer ownership of who he was, no matter the situation. He accompanied him to a small but neat apartment filled with books and, surprisingly, cigars. Charles popped one in Donnie's mouth but didn't light it, then pulled it out only to press his fingers between Donnie's lips. "Use me," Donnie heard himself say, not sure where the words had come from. Charles pushed him down on the ground and whipped out his own cock, which was big, thick and impressive. Donnie's was smaller, but he wasn't jealous, just eager. "I'm clean," Charles said, and Donnie nodded, like he'd been expecting that, though he hadn't been.

Charles held his cock out, then started stroking it. "I'm glad it was you I got to dance for," he said. "The rest of those guys?

You're better than them." And then Charles pressed the head of his cock between Donnie's lips. Donnie swept his tongue over the head, then moaned at the salty taste. He kept going, and Charles gave him room to explore and let his tongue do the talking. Donnie's dick was pressing against his zipper, but he tried to ignore it as he'd only expected to be receiving, not giving: deep throat. "Yeah, take it all," Charles said, and started fucking his face. The moment Donnie thought those words— *He's fucking my face*—he started to lose it. He'd never come before without touching himself but it was about to happen, and he wrapped one hand over Charles's and used the other to release his zipper. Then he simultaneously jerked off and took Charles as deep as he could.

"That's it, frat boy, be a good little cocksucker," Charles murmured, and soon, before Donnie could fully prepare, Charles was shooting down his throat. "Yeah," Charles said, but in Cherry's voice. Moments later, Donnie came all over his hand and his pants, but he didn't care. He made sure to swallow every drop of Charles's jizz and was a little sad when the other man finally removed his cock from his mouth.

"You were wonderful," Charles said, smiling. "I think you should forget about that frat, though."

"Maybe," Donnie told him. So much had changed—or had it? Was he still the same person, just with a hankering for cock? "I better go," he said, suddenly feeling awkward.

"I understand. Maybe I'll see you around sometime," Charles said, going to the bathroom. While his host peed, Donnie pulled himself back together, determined not to burden Charles any more than he had. When they kissed good-bye, he was sure he tasted cherry on his first lover's lips. He smiled as he exited the building and decided to take the long way home. He had a lot to think about.

LESSONS FROM THE LIBRARY

Rick Archer

Drunken frat guys—they were everywhere. Saturday night's performance was like clockwork, probably worse, because even a clock runs slow now and then. By eight P.M. every Saturday, the campus would be filled with men half in the bag, stumbling to the dining hall for a last-minute filler-up, or looking to find another raging pre-party before the actual festivities began. I ran into a few on my way to the library, but none I would want to stop and talk to.

Then Jason crossed my path.

"What's up, stud?" he asked, holding back a hiccup. I stopped short on the sidewalk with my backpack on my shoulder, oblivious to everything but his chiseled chin and his dark brown eyes.

"Heading to the library," I said. "I've got to take a make up quiz tomorrow morning." He looked at me with a half-drunk smile and rubbed my shoulder. I tried to conceal the shudder he gave me, but he was so drunk I doubted he noticed.

"You know, you don't look much like a dweeb. Besides there's a month left in the year. You really should come over to the house sometime."

I pushed the thoughts of where that could lead out of my mind.

"I guess I just don't mesh well at crazy parties," I said. "Little too rowdy for me."

"Sometime soon, huh? You're a good guy, Brian. We miss seein' you out there. Good studyin'," he said, stumbling away toward some destination that involved more booze and half-naked girls. I watched his broad body in tight khaki pants and bright green polo shirt strut down the sidewalk and felt that stir in my groin. I shoved it all out of my mind and headed on toward the library.

It was barren. Not even the front desk had a body behind it. The sun through the bay windows on the first floor had finally set, leaving the area aglow in orange light. I often wanted to scream, or yell or throw my clothes off and do a dance on one of the study tables during that strange sunset hour when the sounds of laughing and the smell of alcohol floated across campus, stimulating my senses. The library was my refuge from nights of debauchery and alcohol, from a past that never left me behind.

"Hello!" I yelled. "HELLO!" My own echo responded, and I couldn't help but giggle. "HELLO!"

"Hello already!" a voice called back. I let out a squeak of surprise. A face popped out from behind a bookcase. It was one I slightly recognized, but I didn't mind. He was gorgeous. His hair was parted down the middle, a golden brown color that shined in the orange glow. He had pale skin, and lips that looked naturally red even without the sun shining on his face. As I got closer to him, his green eyes stared lovingly in my direction.

"I...didn't realize someone was in here."

"No worries," the young man said. "I assumed it would be empty too."

"It usually is."

He stepped out from behind the bookcase, looking just like Jason, except in blue instead of green: a tall frat guy with books in his hands. Or perhaps an athlete? Either way, he looked more familiar as I got closer.

"Hey, uh...Brian, right? In my economics class?" he asked.

"Oh, right," I said, feigning recognition.

"Man, how'd you do on that quiz on Monday?"

"I'm taking it tomorrow, actually. I missed class."

"Want some hints?" he asked.

"That's all right," I said, managing a laugh. I felt his eyes staring into me. "So, what exactly are you doing here then?"

"You want me to leave?" he said with a smile. *God no, not when you smile like that,* I thought.

"No, I'm just surprised."

"I needed a night off from the partying," he said. "And I think my roommate needs the room tonight, you know?"

I wanted to say, *Of course, that's how it is in college.* But I just nodded.

"I guess I'll get out of your hair," he said.

"Well, actually, if you want to help me study a little...it'd be nice." His smile faded with the sun, and he looked at me a moment. He seemed hesitant. Did he see through me? That I didn't need his help to ace a simple quiz? Did he know I just wanted a little eye candy?

"Yeah. All right. I can't go home for a while anyway. I know a good spot on the fourth floor."

I followed behind him as we walked up the stairs. He talked a lot along the way, about being scared, like me, of having only one more year after this before facing the real world. About how his roommate usually stayed with his girlfriend, but this time she would be staying at his place. About how much drinking he'd been doing and how he felt he had earned a little rest.

"The guys would kill me if they knew I was hanging out in the library at night though," he said when we reached the fourth floor. I stared at him with a smile that seemed to make him uneasy. "I'm Aaron, by the way," he added.

"Good to meet you," I said with a laugh.

"I talk a lot."

"I don't mind. What guys?"

"Just some friends of mine. They're still looking to pledge a fraternity next year and we've been out every night this semester."

"I didn't know you could pledge as a senior," I said, feeling any hopes deflate. The idea of drunken frat guys getting a little curious was a myth I had learned about firsthand. Still, he wasn't a frat boy yet...

He led me to a back corner where the periodicals were stacked and covered in dust. This area of the fourth floor was away from any windows or sunsets, but also devoid of any charm. The library staff shoved the microfiche and other less looked at materials here, as well as the smaller tables and awkward chairs.

"Perfect little study area. It's usually empty during the day. I can only imagine what a ghost town it is on a Saturday night," Aaron said. He cleared his throat. I was making him nervous, and could only imagine the rumors he'd already heard about me.

"Sounds okay to me."

We sat down across from each other and opened our books. I read over the same page a few times, listening to the dust settle on the stacks. Aaron made no noise, no indication that he was even breathing. The sounds of laughing and drinking were far in the distance and unable to penetrate the little bubble of solitude we had made.

"So," he said. It was so sudden and loud in the quiet that I jumped. He paused before continuing. "I heard a rumor."

Christ. Here it comes. My thoughts ran to just how I would stop this kid from beating the guts out of me if he wanted to. I might as well have been in the North Pole for all the good shouting would do if it came to that.

"Oh?" I managed to say with cotton mouth.

"Is it true?"

"Is what true?"

"What they say happened at the Sigma Phi House?"

"What do they say happened there?"

Aaron looked nervous. I noticed sweat had broken out across his smooth brow.

"That you hooked up with one of the brothers there. Got caught doing it."

"No way," I said with a slight laugh. It didn't sound like a laugh though. More like a hoarse bark. The rumor persisted everywhere I went. It hung on the lips of everyone who spoke to me and wanted to ask, was in the stare of everyone who looked at me and thought it over in their heads. But my answer was always, "Of course not."

"So you're not gay?"

"Why are you asking me this?" I said. My voice grew louder. It sounded like a scream.

"I'm sorry, I didn't mean to pry. I just…wanted to know if it was true."

I stared into his gorgeous green eyes. I could feel my own body sweating. I wondered if this kid was going to run down the steps yelling that he'd gotten the truth out of me despite my lie, or leap across the small table and beat me up like the kid who caught me with his brother had attempted to do. I'd wrestle him down first if I had to, even if he was good looking.

"Kiss me," he said.

My heart seemed to stop dead. My head spun. I didn't even know what to say, let alone know how to respond. His face was expectant, but when he saw me freeze his face slowly turned to one of horror.

"You're really not, are you?"

"You want me to kiss you?"

"Yes."

"Why?"

"Cause I'm queer, Brian. And I heard the rumor you were too. And if I spent any more time alone wondering where all the other fags on this campus were, I'd go crazy."

I wanted to reach out and grab him; shake him by his stupid colored shirt with the collar sticking up; ask him what took him so long to say something. But I just sat there. Because I knew I was exactly the same. Only when I had tried what he just had, it blew up in my face.

He leaned across the table, pressed his lips against mine and whispered, "Aren't you tired of being alone here?"

"Of course," I said. We kissed again. I pulled away from his soft lips and got up from my seat. Our eyes were locked while I straddled him in his seat, my growing erection pressing against my boxers. I could feel the lump in his own khakis as I settled on him, putting both my hands behind his head and drawing his face toward my own. Our tongues danced together, soft wet kisses that sounded like explosions in the quietness of the library. His hands found their way to my shirt, pulling it over my head and breaking the kiss only for a minute while I did the same to him. His abs were pale but rock hard. The rest of his chest was smooth, his nipples tasting sweet when I nibbled them gently with my teeth. His warm hands ran up and down my back, grabbing at my skin and reaching the back of my head, pulling me in for another kiss.

I slipped off the chair and knelt down, my hands quickly undoing his belt buckle. His dick was straining to get out. In silence he lifted his bottom to allow me to slip his pants off. They came easily, and his dick sprung into the air like an animal released from its cage. It was a modest six inches or so, smooth and pale, with just a tuft of blond hair around the base. It throbbed as I got closer to it.

"It's my first time," he said under his breath.

"Oh."

"I'm sorry."

"You want me to stop?"

"God, no."

I licked along the shaft and his cock bounced. I giggled and then took the head into my mouth. A slight gasp escaped his lips, turning into a moan as I bobbed my head up and down slowly, putting a little pressure on the pink head, my left hand cupping his balls, my right thumb twirling about on his nipple. I worked on him for a few minutes, applying pressure and then backing off, hearing him breathe heavily after a moment or two.

"I want you to do me," he said. I took my mouth off his cock, my jaw a bit sore (it had been a while since I'd given head).

"I don't know if that's a good idea. If it's your first time..."

"Please," he begged. The two of us stood up. He stepped out of his pants and rummaged through the back pocket, pulling out a condom. I was suddenly aware of how naked we were in the library. "Here."

I undid my own belt and slid my pants down, my erection now its full seven inches. He looked down at it like it was pure gold, then swallowed hard. I gave him a quick kiss and turned him around, pressing him down and against the table. I put the condom on, spread his asscheeks, and pressed toward his virgin hole.

"Ow."

"Hang on." I spit into my hand and lubed my cock up, which was ready for anything at this point. With a thrust I pushed inside, hearing him grunt a little, then pushed farther. It took a while to get in, but the warmth and tightness made it worth it. I pulled out, then pushed back in, and soon we found ourselves in a rhythm, my hands on his hips, his hands on the desk, his face clenched in pleasure and pain and his cock slapping against the desk as we did the deed.

With a few more grunts and finally a shudder he came, his asshole clenching tightly around my cock as I pumped him, the tightness and the whole situation just being too much. From deep inside I felt my own orgasm surge through my loins and send spurt after spurt of hot cum into the condom. His cum covered the side of the desk. Neither of us moved for a moment. The sweat glistened on his strong back, and I kissed it lightly. It was salty and delicious.

I pulled out of him gently, and he turned to kiss me.

"Haven't done that in a while," I said. "I hope you enjoyed it for a first time."

"There's the evidence," he said, pointing to the cum. There was certainly no shortage of it. "There's a bathroom down the hall." I gave the condom carefully over to him, and he returned quickly with a batch of paper towels, still out of breath from fucking.

The two of us sat on our backpacks side by side, arms touching, still naked. It was as though we had run a marathon, and were left sweaty and panting, just stopping against a bookcase to relax. My balls were recharging, my spent cock hanging limp in the cool air. There was no sound but our own breathing, rapid but slowing to normal.

"Thanks," he said after a moment.

"Thank *you*."

"What for?"

"For being brave. For saying something."

"I'll admit, I was nervous as hell," he said with a laugh. "I half expected you to punch me in the face. Run around campus calling me queer."

Painful memories stung at my insides like needles. "I know what that's like."

He only nodded. "What do we do now?"

"We should get dressed."

"I mean after that," he said, elbowing me softly.

I shrugged. My mind was still blank. A part of me wanted to ask if there was time for a late dinner before we actually studied. A bigger part of me wanted to just run away and pretend the encounter had never happened. Wouldn't that be easier? Coming out to one person was one thing. Coming out to three thousand students?

"I'm getting cold," I said.

We stood up, my legs and abs suddenly sore, and we dressed silently. The sex had been good, even if it was his first time. It had been a full year since the last time I was with someone, so it had felt like my first time again as well. It felt so good to be close to someone...but now it suddenly felt awkward. What if someone had come in? What if someone had seen?

"No one saw us," he said, as though reading my mind.

"What?"

"Are you worried?"

"I don't know."

"Don't be," he said, leaning in and kissing me once again.

God, it felt good. "I'm good at keeping a secret. Clearly."

"You don't know," I said, "what it's like. Maybe you will. You got lucky tonight. If I hadn't been what you were expecting... things could have been bad."

"I know," he said softly. "I'm sorry about what happened to you."

"I don't want that for you. Not in this environment. Not if you want to get into the frat you like."

"So this will have to be a one-time thing, huh?" he asked. I could hear the hurt in his voice. He sounded like a very naïve, very stupid kid. I felt my anger grow.

"You should be glad. *You* don't have a reputation to rebuild."

He looked down and nodded. Maybe I had hurt his feelings. Probably so, but at the moment who cared? It was true.

I gathered my books, and we walked out together. I wouldn't get any more studying done there, I knew. And when I returned to my dorm alone, the sounds of partying in the distance as I walked home, I realized I wouldn't get any studying done anywhere.

The rest of the week went by with more than the usual seven days, it seemed. I received only one text from Aaron that week, asking how my quiz had gone. I earned a B+, mostly because I couldn't focus on it. The rest of my studies were equally torturous. Nothing seemed interesting. I would read pages of a textbook, then reread the same page over and over with not a single word sticking to the walls of my brain. All I thought about was the library, of my tongue dancing with Aaron's, of his moans as I spread his asshole wide and popped his cherry. Of whether it would happen again.

I was surprised by a second text message that following

Saturday afternoon even though I shouldn't have been. It was Aaron, wondering if I would be "studying" later that night in the library. My loins stirred, but I let the message sit in my phone unanswered most of the day. Jason—lovely, sexy, frat-guy Jason—had offered to let me into his frat party that night. I had already accepted. It was my chance to get in on the good side of campus, maybe hang with the cool kids. Maybe some girl would find me attractive. I didn't know what I'd do with her if she did, but it would look good. And as lonely as I was, I wanted to be accepted. Aaron would thank me later, when his potential frat brothers accepted him as the macho, woman-loving stud they assumed he was.

I was dressed in the brightest polo shirt I could find (red) and a pair of khakis. Campus was small, and after a few short minutes passing a drunken stumbling couple, I walked up to the steps of Jason's fraternity, where three of the older guys sat on the porch, beers in hand. The porch light above their heads cast a low glow around them, making them look like candles in a dark window—not very friendly candles.

"We help you?" one asked.

"Jason said there was a party tonight." The three of them looked at one another, then at me. The sounds of laughter and music thudding from the basement were muffled but audible. "He invited me," I added.

"I guess so. Have a good time," said the tall one by the door. He pushed it open and I darted inside. The hallway led both up and down, the distinct smell of beer wafting from the bottom of the stairwell. I headed in that direction and found another door leading into a dark, rectangular basement that was flooded with bodies. The heat was extreme, and everyone was pressed solidly together, trying to dance and find the beer keg and anyone they happened to be looking for all at once. The men were dressed exactly like me, the girls in skimpy tank tops and shorts, though the darkness made it tough to see anyone.

I felt a tap on my shoulder. Jason spun me around and laughed, yelling something I couldn't hear.

"Hey," I yelled back. He made a motion to his ear and shook his head. He handed me a beer, already open, and took a swig out of the can in his hand. With a laugh and a shrug, I did the same.

The party went on the same way for what seemed like days. People were dancing, laughing, playing drinking games in one corner. A few girls came up to me and offered to dance, though I laughed most of them off. I scanned the crowd every so often to see if Aaron was perhaps nearby, but the sea of lavender and pink shirts all looked the same. He could have been two feet in front of me in the darkness and I'd never have known.

I was standing alone by the end of the night, the room clear of everyone but the brothers, who seemed to have no problem with me, and the girls they would likely be bedding. They were all drunk, hanging off one another, making kissing motions and often missing one anothers' faces. I was having trouble standing myself, but I made sure to keep my eyes on the girls and not on the boys, whose shirts had either come off or were stuck so close due to sweat that I could see all their rippling muscles.

When the music stopped the ringing in my ear continued. The lights were finally on and the brothers began to vanish with their prizes.

"Need a room?" Jason asked, coming up to me with a short blonde by his side. The girl looked at him the entire time with half-closed eyes, one arm around his waist, the other on his chest. "Where's your girl?"

"What girl?" I asked.

"The one who was hanging around you."

Maybe there was one and I hadn't noticed. I looked around but was alone now.

"Ah, better luck next time, eh?" he said, holding a belch in. "I'll see you tomorrow I hope, eh? I'm heading up to watch a movie or something."

The girl giggled and began leading him away. I threw my half-empty can of beer onto the disgusting, liquid-soaked floor and stumbled up the dank stairwell into the cool spring air. The guards outside the porch were gone. Only the light breeze and a few crickets were my companions in the darkness.

I pulled out my phone and attempted to text Aaron, asking where he was. It was nearly 2:45 in the morning. My heart beat wildly at the hope that he'd still be awake.

Drunk came the reply a few moments later.

Want to meet me at my place?

OK, he wrote back.

I walked a little slower, not wanting to get back to my dorm building before him. When I arrived, he stood outside my building with his hands in his pockets, a drunken half smile on his face.

"What's up?" he said with a slight slur.

"The party ended. Everyone went home," I said.

"Same here. It's a bit chilly out here though."

"Want to come in?" I asked.

"Okay."

We were kissing before the front door of the building even closed, and I was rubbing his chest, his back, tousling his hair. I wanted him close. I needed him close. I barely knew the kid, but he was all I had thought about for a week, and the only one I'd been close to in a year. I didn't really care if anyone was in the hallway, even though it was empty. I grabbed his hand and practically dragged him into my dorm, which consisted of two single rooms and a common area. I fumbled with my key in the lock until it was finally open. The two of us stumbled forward in the dark, threw my bedroom door open and slammed it shut behind us.

His shirt was off in a moment; mine was off before I even realized it. His hands were everywhere: my chest, my back. His lips were on my neck, my abs, back to my lips. We were probably making a ton of noise that my roommate might hear, but it seemed like he was far away. All there was were our feelings in the dark. My pants were off. I could feel his hard-on pressed against my own, our bodies squishing them between us as we tried to kiss closer and closer.

"The bed," I managed to mumble.

I threw Aaron down onto my bed without bothering to pull down the covers. The world spun in a drunken swirl, and soon I was on my back, Aaron's hot mouth around my shaft. I felt his teeth scrape a bit, but generally he did well for a first-timer. I got shivers through the tip of my cock all the way up my spine as he worked his tongue up and down, and my balls tightened at the slurping sounds in the dark. He was getting better just in the brief time his mouth had been around my pole.

He came back up and kissed me, swirling some precum between our tongues.

"God, Brian you taste delicious."

"So do you."

"Do you want to fuck me again?"

"Of course."

"Got any condoms?"

I fumbled in the nightstand beside the bed until I found an unopened wrapper, trying furiously to open it without tearing what was inside. He waited patiently while I unrolled the condom over my cock. It was as hard as ever despite the alcohol, and after pulling some lube from my drawer I was well prepared to slide inside him. He turned over and got on his hands and knees, baring his ass for me.

Careful to balance myself despite the spinning, I pressed my cockhead forward and slipped inside of him easily. He grunted all the same, but it was not one of pain. The tightness in his ass felt delicious. Slowly we rocked together until I was deep enough to really start pumping, and he arched his back and worked himself on me even better than he had the week before in the library. My hands gripped his sides tight, in case I lost my balance, but at the rate we were going, neither of us would last long. The warmth and the gripping on my cock were causing my balls to surge. Aaron used one hand to jerk himself as my meat pumped his ass.

"Jesus!" he screamed, jerking furiously. I felt the contractions from deep inside him as he came, hot creamy spurts of cum forming pools on my bed.

"I'm coming soon," I said, clenching my teeth. To my surprise Aaron pulled off of my dick and spun around, yanking the condom off and jerking me the rest of the way to orgasm, my cum hitting him in the mouth and the cheek. I collapsed beside him, hot and exhausted. I felt him kiss me in the dark, and tasted my own cum on his lips. He said something about the covers, and then I heard him laugh. Without thinking, I pulled him close, gave him another kiss and promptly fell asleep.

I awoke to soft kisses on my forehead. Light stung my eyes, and I shook the kisses away. The world was spinning, and it felt as though a vise was squeezing my temples.

"Good morning," said the voice behind the lips that continued kissing. "How do you feel?"

"Terrible."

"At least it's Sunday. No need to rush anywhere," Aaron said. The sunlight filtering through my window lit his features with angelic rays. He looked great even with his hair a mess and little black circles under his tired eyes.

"I don't think I could if I wanted to."

"Want something to drink?" I nodded yes, pressing my hand against my head. He went into the common area without even bothering to find his shorts, coming back buck naked with a glass of water.

"My roommate not around?" I asked after taking several sips.

"I heard him leave this morning early."

"He usually goes for a run."

"That's good."

He sat on the bed and looked at me a little sadly. Or maybe I just looked as bad as I felt and he couldn't help but notice.

"What?" I asked.

"I was surprised you called me."

"Yeah, well. I was just curious what you were up to." It sounded lame even to me. He put his hand on mine.

"I was lonely too. It's not a big deal."

"Sure it is," I said, finishing the water.

"Why are you so afraid of me?"

"I..." My head was killing me. All I wanted to do was sleep, even with this gorgeous, muscular young man sitting on the edge of my bed with his wonderful penis a few inches from me. "Because I don't want you to go through what I did. What I am."

"What do you mean?"

"Defending your reputation. Struggling for your future brothers' approval. They won't let you into a frat if they know you're banging guys in your spare time."

"You don't know that," he said.

"They didn't let me in. I'm finally allowed back into some parties."

"Maybe those parties aren't worth going to, if you can't be yourself."

I lay back on the bed. It was like the truth had socked me backward. Even after going to the party, I had ended up alone. I was too hungover to even remember if I'd had a good time or not.

"I'm not saying we should march down the street holding hands and make out in the cafeteria. But you don't have to keep hiding everything. Not if you know it's what you like. Or need." I looked up at him. His hand was still on mine. I wanted to punch him in the face. Instead I sat up and kissed him. He kissed back.

"You'll get there," he said.

"With a little help," I said. He smiled, gently pushed me back, and we made love in the sunlight.

THE OTHER WHITE MEAT

Gregory L. Norris

He towered over them, terrifying and magnificent in equal doses. Brett Everly made another slow circle around the three young men, saying nothing, the absence of words grunted or shouted into their faces far more effective. The college senior wasn't dressed in the tired cliché of hooded cassock and sandals, but instead wore his football uniform, which was dirty from the team's last game; likely ripe, too. Brett hadn't shaved for at least a day, Crete guessed, maybe two. Rough prickle coated his chin, cheeks and throat, creating the perfect face for football and frat business with freshmen.

"Listen up," Brett eventually said, after reaching the end of his revolution.

His voice, a masculine baritone, launched a shudder down Crete's spine, half out of fear, the rest because that voice excited him despite their present roles of master and mastered.

"I'm disgusted to say that you're the lowliest, ugliest group of poor excuses for Alpha-Zeta-Sigs I've ever seen. Probably the worst *ever*."

Brett sighed. Crete felt the breath rain down cool against the naked flesh of his shoulder and tried to not think about how aroused that one tiny connection left him.

"*Crete*. What kind of a fuckin' name is that? You *cretin*." The master hawked up a wad of spit and let it fly. Brett's DNA struck a different section of his shoulder. It lay there, warm and clotting.

Crete's cock pulsed. Embarrassment sent another shudder into motion, only this one was internal and unpleasantly hot. It tickled him behind the balls, punched him in the guts. What if Brett or the others noticed? Crete, Woodford, and Landen were on the floor, positioned in a human-form triangle, their faces facing out, naked except for their tight whites, boxers and, in Crete's case, gray boxer-briefs, so the fear of being found out was valid.

Brett moved on, focusing his righteous anger on Sloane Woodford.

"Sloane? What kind of name is that? Huh, *Slunt*?"

From the cut of his down-turned eye, Crete drank in Brett's magnificence. He stood just over the six-foot mark, a modern young man of twenty-two with the body of an ancient Greek deity. Big feet in dirty cleats scraped across the wooden floor. Clean white socks rose up to lengths of bare, hairy legs, just beneath the knees. The meaty fullness of Brett's crotch was clearly showcased in the front of his uniform pants. Farther up, there was the trim, muscular torso, a thatch of dark chest hair poking up from the top of his football jersey, and that face, so painfully handsome with its mean blue gaze and neat athlete's brush cut.

"Landen. You ever live on the prairie, homo? In that *Little House of Fairies*?"

"No, Sir, I'm from the Northwest."

"*What?*" Brett barked in response. "Did you just speak? Did I give you permission to?"

Landen shrank in response to their new master's shouts. The other members of the Alpha-Zeta-Sigma Fraternity, also dressed in their football uniforms, chuckled and grunted insults.

The scrape of Brett's gigantic feet—size twelves or thirteens, Crete assumed—again cycled closer. Crete's pulse galloped. Soon, very soon, he would again fall under the watch of the football team's star quarterback. Electricity crackled along the shaft of his dick and around the chin of his cock's helmet. It didn't help that his eyes again went automatically to the crotch of Brett's uniform pants. The cloth behind the laces was thick and swollen, and tight enough to identify shaft, head and both balls. Dare he think it? Was pledging the three freshmen giving Seaside U's biggest man on campus a bone?

"What the fuck are you looking at, dick-breath?" Brett demanded.

Crete deflected his gaze back down to the floor. Seeing Brett's cleats didn't lessen his burden. On a memorable recent Indian summer afternoon, he'd seen Brett strutting around the Alpha-Z-Sig house in a ripped T-shirt, khaki shorts, no shoes or socks. The dude's legs were amazing, perfectly muscled without being showy, and covered in a dark pelt. His feet matched the rest of the man: big, with well-shaped toes and trimmed nails. For reasons he couldn't imagine, Crete had thought nonstop about sniffing Brett's feet and licking between his toes. The space inside those well-worn spikes was, he imagined, a sweaty wonderland. Crete's dick puffed, pulsed.

"Fuckin' cretin," Brett said. "What's this I hear about you not eating meat? You're a fuckin' vegetarian, you pathetic excuse for a sac of nuts?"

Eyes lowered, Crete waited and stared at the big spikes and

sweat socks in front of him.

"Am I talking to the fuckin' walls? I asked you a question, Cretin."

Crete forced his eyes up. "Sir?"

"I asked you if you're a salad shooter, you useless cock-smooch."

Crete choked down a painful swallow. Brett's handsome, heartless face hovered above him. The mastered caught a hint of the master's scent on his next desperate sip of breath—fresh male sweat, clean and piney, the smell of rainstorms and masculine hormones secreted through blood, skin. Finding his voice took Herculean effort.

"Sir, yes, I am a vegetarian."

Brett gazed around the room at the other fraternity brothers, the other football jocks. "You believe this shit?" Then he shot a harsh look at Crete. "We eat meat, Cretin. We're men. American men. Beef, pork, chicken, and turkey in November. Bacon, dude, not *fakon*. You eat bacon, douche?"

"No, Sir, I don't," Crete answered.

Laughter sounded around the room. The glop of Brett's spit sat cold on his shoulder now, a counterpoint against how hot he felt everywhere else. Sweat clung to his armpits and dripped from behind his balls. It struck Crete that the wetness in his underwear might be something other than perspiration—precum—and his pulse quickened.

A mean smile broke on Brett's lips. "You are something fuckin' else, Cretin. What the hell were we thinking when we opened the door and let you into the place? I figure someone who sucks on carrots and cucumbers with such gusto must at least love the occasional hot dog. You like snacking on wieners, Cretin?"

"No, Sir," Crete said. It was as much a lie as it was the truth.

The kind of wiener he craved had little to do with snouts and meat byproducts, and everything with the man demanding an answer.

Brett grabbed hold of Crete's chin, ran a thumb along his lips and forced open his mouth. "You look like a sausage smoker to me."

Brett's thumb rolled over his tongue. Suddenly, all Crete could think about was how much he wished it was Brett's dick, and how badly he wanted to suck it. The thumb was there, penetrating between his lips, fucking his face, all too briefly. Brett moved on, back to Woodford, to—

"*Slunt*, are you a radish-gobbler, too?"

Sloane hesitated. A jab with the toe of Brett's spike loosened his lips. "Yes, Sir, I'm a radish-gobbler. Fuckin' love them!"

"Fuckin' Slunt, you make me sick. Chewing on lettuce leaves when you could be ripping into a big, juicy steak."

"*Tube steak*," one of the football players laughed, out of Crete's line of sight. He heard the thunderclap of a high five as Brett again moved on to Landen.

"And you, bean-breath? Or is that *cum* on your breath, you tree-hugging, granola-eating creampuff?"

"Yes, Sir."

Brett circled back to Crete. The smile on the master's face was beyond mischievous. It both chilled and boiled Crete alive. "Bring the shit out."

The *shit* came carried on a tray. The summer smell of cookouts and hot, lazy days surrounded the bearer: hot dogs, roasted on a grill.

"You want into Alpha-Z-Sig, you got to be a meat eater, like the rest of us, not some fuckin' herbivore. Who's up for a little beef in their diet?"

Crete felt Landen shift beside him, the other pledge's butt

touching against his tense thigh. *The first to crack* thought Crete. By the time this was over, he sensed they all would.

"Me," Landen said. "I'll do it."

Brett pulled a hot dog off the tray and aimed it at Landen's mouth. On the pass by his nose, the smell of the meat thickened. It wasn't a bad smell. Strangely, it even made Crete's taste buds water. But meat hadn't touched his lips in years. Even if he was the type who jonesed on burgers and chops, anything he ate would quickly reappear, he knew, given the present state of his stomach.

Crete rolled his eyes to the left and saw Landen not simply eating the hot dog, but sucking on it, the way one does a Popsicle.

"That's right, bean sprout," Brett growled in a lusty voice. "Suck that wiener."

"Damn," one of the other studs drawled, "look at him go to town. Bet he's great at going *down*."

"No doubt." This, from another.

"Swallow it," Brett ordered.

Landen took the hot dog down to Brett's fingertips, regurgitated it whole, and then went back down again. The itch in Crete's boxer-briefs worsened. The electric charge in the air had become something quite different, and quickly. Landen's mouth on the hot dog was fueling the group's excitement. The undercurrent throbbed. Even the smell in the air seemed to thicken, sweat and pine and maleness mixing together, becoming a narcotic cocktail.

"Fuck, you're good. Bet we could rent that mouth of yours out and make a million dollars with it," Brett said. "You a good cocksucker, bean sprout?"

"No," Landen mouthed around the hot dog.

"No? No *what*?"

"No, *Sir.*"

"You piece of shit. Chew your food, dude," Brett said, releasing the hot dog.

Landen choked it down and gagged. This seemed to excite the football players almost as much as watching him gobble it.

"Who's next? Cretin? Slunt?"

Crete didn't respond. He sensed Landen was no longer part of the equation—he'd been broken, had surrendered by eating forbidden fruit and was off the radar screen now. That left him and Woodford still kneeling beneath the sword.

"Am I talking to myself again?" Brett asked. He leaned down and shouted the question on a fine spray of spittle into Crete's face. "Am I?" He repeated it to Sloane louder—and probably wetter, Crete imagined. "You'd better eat this wiener, or I might just drop trou and make you slurp on *this one.*"

Brett gave his crotch a shake. Now more than before, Crete was sure that their master had thrown wood in his uniform pants. Sloane reached for the hot dogs and ate two, chewing them down in short order.

"Looks like we got ourselves a carnivore here in Slunt-face, after all."

More laughter and additional high-fives passed among the frat brothers.

"How about you go slower on the next one," Brett said. He held out a third hot dog, which Sloane—no longer referred to as Slunt—calmly fellated.

He'd done what was expected of him. That only left Crete to follow through. Brett turned toward him, and now all attention was focused on the remaining pledge. Crete wanted to hide almost as much as he wanted to nut. Almost.

"Look at you, you cretin," Brett said, running his eyes down and then back up. "You sick, twisted fuck. That dick of yours looks hard enough to pick my teeth with. And *small* enough. What the fuck?"

Crete swallowed. There was no use denying the charge—not that he'd been given permission to speak, especially in his own defense. He sensed every eye on his crotch, linking the room full of witnesses to the truth, to the proof of his guilt.

"Dude's seriously getting off on this!"

"He's fuckin' stiff!"

"Bet he loves meat more than these other two freshman fucks."

"Yeah, *man-meat*."

Fresh scales of ice formed over Crete's mostly naked flesh. He fought the urge to shiver, but failed. Brett got back in his face. While being berated and humiliated, it struck Crete that he had never seen so handsome a face, so hot a body. Brett Everly was all man, all *cock*.

"You got anything to say for yourself, fuck-tard?"

Crete didn't and shook his head.

"What's wrong—you got a dick in your mouth, dude?"

Brett reached for a hot dog. Crete turned away as it approached his mouth. "No."

"No? *No!*"

"No, *Sir*. I don't eat meat. I don't want it in my mouth."

A terrible silence briefly settled over the room. The absence of sound drummed at Crete's ears.

"You don't?" Brett said. "Maybe you'd rather have my dick in your yap instead."

Crete met Brett's eyes. This time, he didn't look away. In a calm voice, he said, "Sir, yes I would."

"You would? You'd rather suck on my cock than choke down a frankfurter?"

Crete nodded. The room again fell silent, as if no one dared to comment. The rabid sexual tension thickened, while the chaos of Crete's thoughts clarified. He had thrown down the gauntlet and challenged the biggest man on the Seaside U campus to put his money where his mouth was. Or, more accurately, his money in Crete's mouth. To balk would take away his credibility, his power. Brett was an alpha male whose reign was about to either be toppled, or solidified.

Their eyes remained locked. Brett blinked first.

"Fuck," the master huffed, mastered.

A second or two more of indecision followed, and then Brett straightened. He flashed a cocky smirk that said he wasn't going to be bested and reached both hands toward his crotch.

"You crafty fuck, Cretin," Brett said.

No one spoke. Brett opened the laces of his uniform pants and spread the halves apart, baring a foul gray jockstrap stretched out of shape by its owner's hard dick.

In a low, threatening voice, Brett said, "Your move."

Damn the torpedoes, Crete thought, and reached for Brett's junk.

The silence persisted, and Crete imagined the rest of Alpha-Z-Sig's members were too stunned to move. One hand met the top of Brett's pants. The other felt the meaty fullness of his crotch, through his jockstrap. It was no longer a question of imagining the quarterback's excitement; Brett *was* hard. And he was Crete's, at least for the moment.

Crete pulled, tugged. The ripe old jock and Brett's uniform pants came halfway down his butt. His cock log-rolled out, snapped up, and bobbed over two of the fattest, hairiest nuts Crete had ever seen close up. Quickly, he recorded the details of his master's dick: a bone average in terms of both length and thickness, the meaty shaft upwardly curved, with lots of dings and veins; the head a classic fireman's helmet, its single eye weepy with a clear teardrop; all of it above-average because of the man it was attached to. A thick pelt of fur ringed Brett's cock and the two low-hanging nuts beneath it.

The funky stink of balls filled Crete's lungs. Leaning forward, he drew in another full breath, opened wide and took the head of Brett's cock between his lips. He gobbled a few more inches, the salty-sour taste of precum mixed with a real man's sweat igniting on his tongue. Deeper he sucked Brett's shaft, recording the details of texture, scent and the pulsations emanating from within.

Brett groaned a blue streak of expletives, pushed forward and buried the rest of his dick in Crete's face. The master's balls gonged against Crete's chin. Struggling to not gag, Crete opened wider, sucked, and fondled Brett's nuts, loving their looseness and sweaty smell.

"You fuckin' carnivore," Brett huffed.

Crete sucked, tugged. The latter sent Brett to the tops of his toes in his spikes. The taste of precum thickened. The mastered snaked his free hand down and ogled his dick, but as soon as Brett saw what was doing, he discouraged it with a jab from his foot.

"You ain't here to get yourself off," Brett spat. "Make *me* squirt, you cock-loving come-hound."

Crete moaned around Brett's dick, massaging it with vibrations as well as lips and cheek muscles, proving he was more than capable of giving the master what he demanded.

"Fuck," Brett moaned.

Crete looked up to see the other young man's eyes were half closed, his head tossed back, a hard expression on his face. Crete rolled Brett's balls over his chin and nose. Their musty stink spurred him forward with renewed gusto, up and down, his mouth sucking, gulping. Precum flowed. Brett's breaths quickened. The realization that all of the fraternity was watching added another layer of excitement, but to Crete, it was only about the two of them. Brett's cock and Crete's mouth. It was the perfect moment.

Then Brett howled, "Oh, dude, here it fuckin' comes!"

Crete tugged Brett's balls even harder. That did it. A blast of whitewash sprayed the back of his throat. Another painted his tonsils. Sperm flooded Crete's mouth. He swallowed to keep up with the ejaculations, right as Brett threatened him that he'd better not waste any.

"Drink my baby-juice, cocksucker. Oh, yeah, every fuckin' drop."

Crete did as told and cleaned off Brett's cock, which hung red and proud, still hard, out of his football uniform. With that accomplished, he stole several licks off of Brett's balls, out of respect.

"Good job," Brett sighed.

Crete gazed up to see the master's handsome face had the makings of a smile on one edge of his mouth. "Thank you, Sir."

"I'm going to enjoy having you around, Crete."

He was Crete again, one of the brotherhood. But in that acknowledgment, Brett was also the master once more, and the man in charge of keeping order.

"Yes, men, we got ourselves a bona fide boner-lover here. You suck the fuckin' marrow out of it, don't you, Crete?" To drive home the point, Brett choked up on his root and swung, smacking him across the mouth with his still-stiff cock.

Crete licked his lips, loving the taste of Brett's dregs. "Yes, Sir."

"And you know how lucky you were just now to get a big ol' bellyful of Alpha-Zeta-Sig spunk, blasted right down your lowly throat."

"Yes I do, Sir."

The smile on Brett's face widened and again took on its mischievous bent. "Okay, then...who's next?"

The football jocks nearly trampled one another in attempting to get to the head of a very long line.

GIVING IT UP FOR THE HOUSE

Christopher Pierce

I always thought that if you looked up "frat boy" on Wikipedia there should be a picture of Denny. He was archetypal—handsome in a traditional, conservative way with his short, curly, blond hair, sea-glass blue eyes, ample mouth with bright white teeth always grinning or on the verge of doing so; strong, sturdy body but not bulky, sculpted chest with just a few hairs between his pecs, hairy legs and big feet tucked into expensive tennis shoes.

He had been my Big Brother when I'd first pledged Sigma Tau Delta, and during Rush Week he'd learned of my...special talents—mainly, that I was gay and more than happy to sexually service a potential frat brother, especially one as hot as he was.

I was accepted into Sigma Tau Delta.

Denny and I had our little secret, and after I'd gotten into the frat he continued to make use of me whenever he wasn't getting enough from the girls or was sick of jerking off. I wondered if the other brothers were ever suspicious of our late-night study sessions in Denny's room.

Whenever we were alone, Denny would give me a signal: he'd drop his pants or shorts to the floor, revealing his tight white athletic briefs. The promise of those briefs and the glory that waited inside was not something I could ever resist. I came to him immediately, quickly assessing the situation—was he standing up, sitting on a chair, or sometimes assuming more exotic positions like sprawling across a desk or spreading out like a main course on a dining room table.

One night he called me to his room at the Sigma House to study for an exam we both had the next day. After several hours of work I glanced at the clock and saw it was past 2:00 A.M. Denny was sitting across from me, rubbing his eyes.

"I'm sick of studying," he said, slamming his textbook closed and eyeing me like a wolf spotting a little lost lamb. "Get over here."

I gave him a playful smirk as he stood up.

"Come on," he said, "you know you want to."

He was right.

I crawled on my knees across the carpeted floor to him. He shucked off his shorts and now the shape of his long stiff bone showed clearly through the thin fabric of his briefs.

"Are you sure we're alone?" I asked teasingly.

"You saw me lock the door, man!" Denny said in a ferocious whisper, "Now *suck my dick!*"

It was time to get down to business.

But it couldn't be rushed; I had to take my time like I always did. On my knees, I put my face in Denny's crotch and inhaled deeply through my nose. I smelled a sensual blend of musk, sweat and that particular odor of his that I craved day and night. Nuzzling his cock with my nose, I felt the organ shiver, trapped within the tight underwear. I ran my nose up and down the shaft, loving the feeling even through the barrier. I licked his bulge a few times, then put my mouth on it and exhaled strongly.

"Mmm," Denny murmured. I knew he loved that flush of heat, that sensuous preview of the sensations to come. After breathing hard on his dick a few more times, I put my mouth to even better use. Skillfully taking the waistband of his briefs between my teeth, I pulled them up, out and then down, revealing his long, juicy cock. I licked it again, this time directly on the naked flesh.

"Aw, fuck," Denny said above me.

I loved the taste of him, so salty and male. Running my tongue up and down his shaft was incredible as always, an electric sensation that made my own cock stiffen in my pants. I took the head of his dick inside my mouth, gratified by the curse of pleasure my Big Brother let out quietly. I let his cockhead rest on my tongue for a minute, just enjoying the sensation of having it in my mouth. Then slowly I started to caress it with my lips and tongue. Denny groaned above me. Little by little I took in his length, his long dick disappearing into my mouth.

I took as much as I possibly could down my throat, then began to suck in earnest.

I'm a world-class blow job artist, so you shouldn't be surprised to learn that Denny's moaning got loud enough that I had to pound lightly on his chest with my fist to let him know to shut up. I didn't know what would happen if the other brothers found out about us. They'd probably kick us both out of the frat. Denny's answer was to grab my head with both hands and start face-fucking me. He plowed my mouth, shoving his cock as far into me as he could. I loved every second of it. I could tell his intensity was reaching a breaking point—he was just about to come when he pulled my head back. His bone popped out of my mouth with a slurp. I sat back on my knees.

"What the fuck?" I said.

"Goddamn, man," Denny said, "you've got me so hot I gotta fuck you. Stand up and turn around!"

I couldn't have been more pleased. Denny loved fucking my ass—he was good at it—and I loved it when he did it. I did as he said, jumping to my feet and turning away from him so he had the best access to my rear entrance.

"Take off your clothes," Denny told me.

I obeyed, and he took off his shirt after pulling a tube of lube and a condom packet out of his bedside drawer. He put his hands on my hips and said, "Bend over." His voice got all deep and husky when he was about to fuck me.

I obeyed, bending at the waist, my hands reaching for the floor, giving my fuckbuddy his best possible access to my asshole. After I was down, I heard Denny tear open the condom packet and slip the latex sheath over his tool. There was a slurping noise, and I knew he was lubing himself up. Even though I was eager for his dick inside me, my hole has always been tight and needs some encouragement before it gets plowed.

Denny took one hand off my hip and brought it to his mouth, I assumed, because I heard another slurpy noise. Then he gently inserted a slick finger into my asshole. I wanted more and pushed back until his finger was in up to the hilt. With me wiggling my ass he was able to get two more fingers in me.

"You want it bad, huh, man?" he asked.

"You know it, dude," I said, panting, "go ahead and do me."

He popped his fingers out and once again pressed his cock-head to my hole. I flexed and opened to entice him, and he entered me. His mushroom head slid past the ring of muscle around my asshole, and he was in. Now it was just a matter of inches. I wanted to jerk myself off, but told myself to wait and concentrate on Denny's pleasure first. The lube was chilly to begin with, but the heat of his cock and my ass warmed it up nicely.

My frat brother put one hand on each of my hips, holding me in place. I loved having him inside me. Denny got so hard it was like having a broom handle or a steel pipe up my ass. Once Denny had his full eight inches in me, he paused for a minute to just enjoy the sensation of being inside me.

Then, after a few deep breaths, he was ready for action. He started pulling out of me, then pushing back in a few inches at a time. I wasn't in the most comfortable position, leaning over with my butt in the air, but I loved getting fucked by this guy so much it was worth it. He moved his groin sensually, boning me with the skill of a champion. With the erotic familiarity of longtime fuckbuddies, Denny and I found our rhythm quickly, with him thrusting and me pushing back on him. As much as he loved fucking me, though, he could never do it for very long without shooting his load—and soon enough I heard the rapid breathing that signaled he was getting close.

"I'm gonna blow, man!" he said.

"Go ahead!" I urged him. "You know I want it! Give it to me!"

"I'm coming—aarrgghh!" he grunted, and I knew he was shooting a nice big load into the condom inside me. Luckily, when we got together he usually had two or three loads saved up for me, so I knew this was just round one. Little did I know just how many rounds there were going to be tonight.

Denny was just pulling out of me when I heard a key turning in the lock and the door to his room swung open!

"What the hell?"

In the doorway stood Sam Gable, one of the upperclassmen

and a brother I'd always thought was hot.

"Crap!" Denny said, pulling up his shorts and stepping away from me. I just stood there, naked, looking at Sam with a smile on my face and my dick hard as a rock.

"Well, this explains what you two've been doing all these late nights," he said.

"You won't tell the other brothers, will you?" Denny asked him.

"That depends," Sam said, stepping into the room and closing the door.

"On what?"

Sam grinned at me.

"On whether you'll agree to share him with me."

THERE'S SOMETHING ABOUT BRANDON I CAN'T PUT MY FINGER ON

Shane Allison

I had just got off work. I was hungry and sleepy as hell hoping I wouldn't nod off at the wheel on my long drive back to the sticks. As I drove through town, I caught sight of someone I knew. I wasn't sure it was him at first, but the closer I got, the more of him I could make out, and sure enough…it was Brandon Mathis. "Muthafucka!" I smiled. He was clearly drunk off that fine, bubble butt of his, stumbling down the street like some wino. I started to just leave his ass alone, thinking that he would eventually get to wherever he was headed. But then I thought, *What if he gets hit by some drunk kid behind the wheel? Or a bunch of rednecks beat his ass just for the fuck of it?* Either way, I wouldn't have been able to forgive myself. I drove alongside him and let down the passenger side window. "Wassup, Biaaatch!"

He looked into the car at me. "What's up witcha?" His white teeth juxtaposed nicely against his black velvety skin. The peach-hued sheen from the streetlights bounced off his shaved head.

"You want a ride?"

"If you don't mind." He opened the door and got in. I quickly noticed the large blistered symbol on the upper part of his left arm. I had seen the same painful-looking sign before on another brotha's skin. I recognized it as a symbol from one of the local black fraternities on the campus of Florida Southern University, Alpha Omega. I had always meant to ask Brandon about it when he worked at the theater with me, but we hardly said so much as boo to each other.

"Where you comin' from?" I asked.

"I walked my ass all the way from Chubby's, man. They had that Rick Ross concert ova there tonight."

"I know. I wanted to go, but I couldn't get anybody to cover my shift. How was it?"

"Shane, that shit was off the chain."

"Whaaat?"

"He blew it up. RICKY RO-ZAY!" He yelled out of the window.

"I shoulda just called my ass in sick."

"Man, you missed a good-ass show."

"That's why I need to quit that shit. No muthafuckin' social life."

"That's why I left, working every damn weekend, every Saturday night. Is that where you comin' from?"

"Yeah, I just got off.

"You smell like popcorn." I tugged at my shirt and took a whiff. Brandon started laughing. "I'm playin'." The smell of booze and high-end cologne filled my silver SUV.

"So, I heard you quit because of that pencil-dick, Chris."

"That was part of it, but mostly 'cause my grades were takin' an ass-kickin' 'cause of the late hours. I wouldn't get out that bitch until sometimes two in the mornin'."

"So you don't miss it?"

"Hell, no! The free movies, yeah, but not gettin' home late and on top of that, tryin' to study."

I knew Brandon's type: a player, a butch type of brotha who would want to kick your ass if you talked about anything that was remotely gay. I went through high school with dudes like him, the kind that would sit in the back of class and call me faggot and punk-ass bitch; some of those boys only liked me in the woods behind Richards High School when my lips were roped around their dicks.

To say that Brandon is fine as hell would be the understatement of 2011. I was always checking him out, taking glances at his ass. He would come to the theater when he was off, looking much like he looked now in my car: muscles tight under a Hollister T-shirt, a pair of baggy cargo shorts hanging just so, showing a little booty under his boxers. If I didn't know any better, I would think he was doing it on purpose, teasing me with the shit so I would walk around work the rest of my shift on hard. It was like ninth-grade P.E. all over again, when I used to wear an extra pair of shorts under my sweats so no one would notice that my shit was hard. On my break at work, I would haul ass to my car and jack off while thinking of Brandon booty-naked, hovering over me with his dick in my mouth. I thought of how lucky his girlfriend was that she could have his dick whenever the mood struck. But like I said, I *know* types like Brandon. They put on a good show, but behind the closed doors of bathroom stalls, in dark booths of sex arcades, they're quick to let another man get that dick, and the booty too, sometimes. I don't know. There was always something about Brandon I couldn't put my finger on.

"So where you stay?" I asked.

"You can drop me off at the Omega House. You know where that is?"

"Up on FSU campus, right?"

"Yeah, I'll pointchoo to it when we get up there." Brandon kept on talking about the Rick Ross concert. "And man, the girls—fine as fuck." The alcohol on his breath was like a bitch slap in my face.

"Did you get any numbers?"

"Hellz, yeah! This shawty I was standing next to at the concert." Brandon held up his hand to show me that she had written her number on his palm.

I played the shit off like I actually gave a fuck that he met some chicken head. Brandon kept grabbing his junk. I tried not to look, but it's like I'm programmed as a gay man to just zero in on dick, especially when somebody like Brandon gave attention to it. The symbol on his arm should have been enough to keep my eyes off his dick.

"Man, I have wanted to ask you about that right there forever," I said, pointing to it. "That must have hurt like a bitch."

"Hell, yeah, but only for a bit. ALPHA OMEGA FOR LIFE, BABY!" Brandon hollered, as he formed the symbol of his frat with his skinny black fingers.

"How long you been a member?"

"Pledged my sophomore year."

"What made you wanna pledge?"

"Had to keep this shit in the family, man. All my brothers are Alphas. My daddy's an Omega and my granddaddy. Alpha Omegas for life."

"You oughta have that tattooed on your chest somewhere."

"What? *Omega for life?*"

"4 life. You know, a number instead of the letter, like Tupac."

"That's not a bad idea."

"I'm jokin', man."

"No, for real. I might do that shit."

Straight people and the crazy-ass shit ya'll do, I thought. "So what do ya'll do, like sit around drinkin', hazin' brothas and shit?"

"Nah, man, that's what people think, but no. We do throw parties and socials and stuff, but we don't let shit get out of control. We don't haze our brothas. I know frats that do it, but we don't. People have a lot of misconceptions about us. A good frat brotha is a gentleman; you know what I'm sayin'? Leaders in the community."

"I think people have that idea based on what they see in movies."

"And some dudes only pledge 'cause they think all frats do is drink and party, but we, and I speak for all fraternities, we are more than that. Omegas have gone on to be doctors, lawyers, teachers, guys givin' back to the community."

I could see that Brandon was passionate about what he was saying, and sounded hell-bent on squashing the stereotype that was always a pus-filled stigma on fraternities.

"Man, you know what? I respect that. I appreciate you clearin' that up, and I owe you an apology." I held out my hand until ours came together with *dap.*

"That's what we try to do. Educate."

Brandon continued to grab at his crotch as if it were as common as batting an eyelash, pulling at it as if he sought to make room in his shorts due to its length. I wanted him to pull it out. I wanted him to stick it in my mouth. I was done talking. Sleep was no longer on my mind, and I was no longer hungry. Not for food anyway. I wanted to suck Brandon's dick. I wanted him to fuck me. We had reached the campus, slowly cruising past big brick buildings named after historical black

scholars. "It's right up here," he said, veering off the conversation. I pulled into a full lot and parked in front of a huge brick
house. Large Greek letters were posted just above the entrance
of the frat house. I thought of all the hot black men that lived
under its roof who pranced around half-naked behind those
windows. About four guys were sitting out front, looking at us
suspiciously like hungry buzzards, wondering who this guy was
that had driven up in an SUV.

"Damn, this where you stay? Place is huge."

"You should see how it look inside. You want a tour?"

I had never been in a frat house before. I expected the place
to be in shambles: dirty clothes, beer cans, empty pizza boxes.

"It's late. I gotta be at the theater at eleven tomorrow."

"Man, bring yo' ass in here, meet some of the brothers."

The men that were sitting studied me. They were of assorted
tones of black: brown-skinned, dark chocolate, butterscotch-
yellow; brothas with braids, fades and bald to the scalp.

"This is Trey, Big Will, Taj and Mike D. Shane works at the
theater."

"Can you get us some passes?" Mike D asked.

"Just come by the theater. I'll hook you up." Mike D was
one of the cuter ones out of the bunch, with full, pretty lips and
short hair.

When I followed Brandon inside, I saw that it wasn't as dirty
as I'd thought, but it wasn't that clean either. There were a few
guys, but none of them were half-naked. There were hardly any
men around. It was Saturday, so I figured they were out at the
clubs.

"That's the entertainment room where we watch games,
study, whatever, the kitchen, and right there is the bathroom."

As Brandon started upstairs, he kept yanking his shorts up
over his booty, covering plaid boxers. "These are more rooms

and bathrooms and this is my room." Brandon's room was fairly clean. I looked at the bed and thought of all the women that had probably been fucked on it. "Sit anywhere you want. I gotta piss." I sat in the chair at his desk where an open math book lay. Posters of shiny, pricey cars and sports figures plastered the wall. A Rihanna calendar was thumbtacked above Brandon's desk. I soon heard the loud, thick sound of piss splashing in the toilet.

"Oh, hey, you still with whatsherface?"

"Who?

"Ol' girl you use to bring to the movies."

"Janiece? Yeah, we on and off. Mostly off."

"Whatchoo mean?" I asked. I heard a flush and Brandon walked out with the clasp of his shorts undone.

"She trippin', man, talkin' about how I don't spend enough time with her and shit. All she does is nag me. I love her, but damn."

I could see the frustration in his face. Poor Brandon. Poor fine ass, bubble-booty, Rick Ross–loving Brandon.

"You want some to drink? He walked over to the minifridge in the corner of the room.

"Does everyone have one of those?"

"No, my daddy brought this up from Miami." He opened it up and took out two beers. He twisted off the tops and handed me a bottle. We both took a swig. I steered the conversation back to the Alpha Omega symbol on his arm. "What made you want to do that to yourself?"

"I'm a member for life. I wanted something to show my loyalty."

"Yeah, but damn, dog. Why not just wear a T-shirt or somethin'?"

"It's just a part of who I am."

"I read somewhere that branding was a form of ownership during slavery."

"Yeah, but branding goes farther back than that. In Africa, some tribes would brand a boy as he entered into adulthood."

"Well, you're braver than my ass. I would have freaked out. Shit, I never would have even done it."

"When I'm eighty, I want to still look at it." Brandon sat his beer down at the foot of the bed and took off his shirt. *Sweet baby Jesus!* I thought. I tried like hell not to stare. It was like my whole body had gone completely numb. *Roll your tongue back in your head, Shane,* I thought. You could bounce a penny off his chest. Hell, fuck a penny, more like a wrecking ball. Brandon had already had my dick twitching in my black work pants all night, but once he took his T-shirt off, exposing his smooth chest, abs and pecs, I had a full-on rocket ship in my drawers, and there wasn't a thing I could do. I don't know what stopped me from reaching over and laying my hands on this brotha. Maybe it was the fact that he would probably yank my ass up? No, my mama didn't raise no fool. The last time I got close to a body like Brandon's was at Triple X-Mart. It was me, a bi dude and his wife, all of us in a booth. He was this freak-a-leak white boy that wanted his girl to watch while he blew me. I ran my hands along his back and could feel every rippling muscle under his skin. I didn't think my fat ass would ever get another chance to touch a man who was as fine as him. He wanted his wife to suck me off, but she just sat there. I put my hand on her left titty, being that I had never done that before neither. It just felt like a soft mass of flesh. Her nipple felt like a perky cherry. The guy had a big dick. I wondered how well endowed Brandon was.

"I don't think I remember you looking so tight," I said.

"I just started taking care of myself a few months back; doing crunches, and sit-ups, liftin' weights. I lost weight when

I started playing football. I don't eat fast food or fried food. I don't drink sodas and if I drink juice, I get somethin' with not a lot of sugar and shit in it."

"That's what I've started doin'. My problem is snacks and eating late at night where I can't burn it off."

"I got a membership at Gold's. If you wanna come out, start workin' out with me..."

"Yeah, I wanna lose like thirty pounds. I actually wanna see my dick without havin' to tuck in this gut."

Brandon took the bottle of beer and began rolling it against his chest. Did this brotha know what he was doing to me? He had to know that if he kept that up, I was going to explode in my pants.

"So I gotta ask you this."

"Wassup?"

'With all these guys living under one roof, in the same house..." Brandon looked at me like he knew what I was about to ask. "There has to be some gay shit going on."

"Naw, we don't get down like that, man."

"How you know?" Brandon laughed, taking another swig from his beer. "I'm serious. You can't tell me that with all these guys living in a frat house, some of these guys up in here ain't suckin' dick?"

"I know every brother in this house and that ain't how we get down," said Brandon.

"So, you know this for a fact?"

"I wouldn't say for a fact, no, but I would know if somebody up in here was gay."

"Like how?"

"Well, you know how they do. How some of them act like females and shit."

"So that's the telltale sign?"

"I'm sure there are straight-acting gay dudes out here, but the ones I usually see act like bitches." Brandon's ignorance was making my dick go down.

"I just never get used to hearing stereotypes like that."

"Oh, come on, man."

"No, I just hate when people make generalizations. In this day and age you would think people were more sophisticated."

"Just like your *sophisticated* misconceptions about all frat boys being a bunch of beer-guzzling date-rapists?"

"Damn, man, who said anything about rapin' somebody?"

"Think about it: had you not run into me tonight, you still would have gone on assuming that all frat guys do is throw parties and paddle pledges."

"True. You right. I don't want to go away from here and leave you thinkin' we all look a certain way or act a certain way. There's so much more to gay people than whatchoo might think."

"And I can say the same thing about frats," Brandon said.

"Now, you might not know any guys that get down, but I guarandamntee somebody messin' 'round. If you have nothing but dudes living together with no women around and you know how much we think about sex, something is bound to jump off. I mean shit, look at the prison system."

Brandon sat back with his elbows hunched on the bed. "You want another beer?" he asked, getting up to head for the mini-fridge. I was still nursing on the first one he'd given me that had turned warm.

"Don't try to get me drunk," I teased.

"I'm not, just tryin' to get you hungover," he grinned.

He plucked two more beers out of the fridge, popped off the tops and handed one to me. His skinny, pussy-fucking fingers grazed against mine in the hand-off.

"If I do get drunk, work is the last place my ass is going."

"That's the idea," he said.

"So can I ask you something?" *Oh shit*, I thought.

"I use to hear stuff about you at work."

"Well, if they ain't talkin' about you, your ass ain't relevant. What stuff?"

"Well, Kenny said he stopped talking to you because sex is all you talk about on Facebook."

"What? We talk all the time," I laughed.

"About balls?" Brandon asked.

"We have had like—brief conversations about sex. Not gay sex, but just sex in general."

"You like Kenny?" Brandon asked.

"No!" I laughed.

"I'm not going to tell him."

"I don't like him like that, no."

Brandon smiled like he had gotten the best of me.

"Is Kenny gay?"

"Don't think so. He and his ex still kick it."

"'Cause people at work think you like him."

"Well, they way the fuck off."

"Keira said you used to tell her how good I looked."

"Oh, god, what?"

"It's cool, man. I'm actually flattered."

"I'mma kill her."

"So you admit it?"

"You got a nice body."

I was still stuck on the part about Kenny not talking to me. Fuck him, fat little munchkin ass.

"It's not like I never noticed you looking. Don't lie," he smiled. I was sure with the cheap alcohol Brandon had consumed, plus the beers, it was making him lose his inhibitions.

"Since we're being so candid, have you ever thought about it?"

"Thought about what?"

"What it's like to do it, to have sex with a dude?"

"I mean, I've let guys suck my dick before," he said "guys," plural. I was shocked by his confession.

"Have you fucked a guy?"

"In the ass? No."

I took a longer swig.

"Would you?'

"With a rubber, yeah. I ain't tryin' to get shit on my dick."

"You so nasty."

"You got no idea," said Brandon.

He said that as if it were some kind of invitation. My dick was hard again, and I could see a little pop tent in Brandon's shorts. I decided to play it off like I wasn't interested. "I need to get going. It's really getting late." I took a long final drink and sat the empty bottle on the desk.

"So, that's wassup? You just going to leave me with blue balls?" Brandon started tugging at his crotch. I watched him rub his dick through his shorts. *Don't even act like you don't want to hit that,* I thought. I didn't say a word, but just walked back in front of Brandon, dropped to my knees between his legs, unzipped him, and reached through the slit of his red and white boxers and pulled out his dick. The thing was like a baby's arm; he was hung like a stallion. The head of his dick was a pretty cashew nut-brown while the shaft was of a nice ebony hue. I pulled his shorts and boxers down to his ankles. His balls, which weren't as big, sat in his lap like a dime bag. I brought the head to my mouth and eased it past my lips, making them tight around the dick head and shaft. I started sucking Brandon's dick. This was it; the thing I had often fantasized about during morning jack-off sessions was actually happening. There he was, sprawled out like a birthday gift to me on his bed. I looked up at him as I sucked. I wanted him to see how I looked with his dick in my mouth. Guys like that kinda shit.

"Deep," he said.

I slid down until his whole dick was in my mouth, until his pubic hairs tickled my nose.

"Suck it." I started to feel Brandon's hands creeping along the back of my neck and then up behind my head. He pressed me down on his dick. "LaDarien said you could suck dick."

What? That muthafucker told? I don't know why I was surprised. Of course LaDarien told him that we fucked around. Those two are thick as damn thieves. Brandon was not forceful like most guys I've been with who just wanted to hold my head down on it. It's like they forget there's a guy attached to the mouth that's sucking them. I acted like I was making love to his dick. When I reached up and started playing with his nipples, he went bananas. I could feel his dick ballooning in my mouth. I hugged it with my lips.

"Yeah, like that, damn!" As I blew him, I heard a creak at the door. My eyes met the sound. Brandon continued to lie there, so obviously he heard nothing. He had forgotten to lock it. I couldn't make out who was standing there, but I liked that I was being watched. Had Brandon known, he would have gone ape-shit. I put on a show by starting to moan. I pulled off Brandon's kicks, slipped his shorts and boxers off to the floor from his socked feet. The covers bunched beneath him as he slid up into the bed, his dick sopped with my spit. When I told him I wanted him to fuck me, he said, "I don't want to get shit on my dick."

"That's what I mean, with a condom. You got some?" I asked.

Brandon got out of bed, walked to his desk and got a couple of rubbers. I could feel the stranger's eyes on me, watching me get undressed, my ass in his face, my hard dick in his view. Brandon tore open the cellophane, took out the lubricated latex and rolled it slowly onto the head of his dick, down his hard shaft. The tips of his fingers were greasy from the lubricant. I lay on my back, exposing my asshole, but Brandon, said, "No, I like it doggy-style." I really didn't care what position I was in, as long as I was going to get fucked by Brandon Mathis. I thought, *This is always how it is with you so-called "straight boys": always gotta be in control, always gotta be the one "on top." You're not gay if you the one doing the fucking, right? Your masculinity and heterosexuality is still well fucking intact as long as I'm sucking your dick. What a crock of shit.*

The guy watching was good about keeping quiet. It still had not occurred to Brandon to check if the door was locked.

I felt his skinny fingers pull at my right asscheek, and cool air kissed my core. Brandon began to press hard against me. I could feel the blunt crown of his dick being worked between the crack of my booty. I looked to the peeping stranger as Brandon slid slowly inside me. I could feel his washboard stomach graze against my booty. He held on hard to my hips as he thrust, and I groaned softly, staring directly at the stranger as Brandon dicked me down. I wanted him to stumble in and pretend to be surprised, say something stupid like, "Oh, I didn't know anyone was in here." You know, play it out like it was some kind of over-the-top gay porn movie. I didn't care if it was one or a hundred frat boys standing there. I wanted them to see their brother Brandon fucking me, fucking another *man*. "Take it deep!" I said. Brandon's hands were warm. The guy in the doorway caressed the tent in his shorts.

"Come here," Brandon whispered. He slid his dick out of me.

What was he doing? He lay flat on his back, his rubber-covered dick sticking straight up from his lithe, chocolate physique. I leaned back against his dick as he slid it steady back up my hole. "Ah, fuck!" he moaned. I rode him steady. I could feel my asshole devouring inch after fat inch as I looked at the horned-up frat boy watching us. I imagined the whole damn house assembled outside Brandon's room, men of all heights, weights and dick sizes waiting anxiously to fuck.

"Goddamn!" Oh yeah, he was close. I spat in my hand and slathered my dick with the stuff, jacking myself off as I slid up and downward on his magic stick. The smell of sweat and booty filled Brandon's room. "I'm comin'! Fuck, I'm..." Brandon released a long groan like it was his last. As I hunched over on my hands, his dick popped out of my booty. "Fuck," he said breathlessly. He got up and walked to the bathroom and ran the shower. I showed the guy standing at the door my fucked but still hungry hole. I continued jacking off while Brandon washed up in the bathroom. I was able to make out more of the man that had been standing there watching us. It was the one known as Mike D, the brotha who had asked me about movie passes. He was caressing his dick through his shorts, licking his lips as he watched me. My suspicions about frat guys messing around with each other had been put to bed so to speak. I had a feeling that I wasn't the only dude Brandon had boned.

I waved him to come in. Two fine ass black men in one night. He walked in and gently closed the door. Mike D looked like a basketball player standing over me. He hooked a few fingers over the elastic of his shorts and pulled out his dick, which was just as big as Brandon's. The shade of his shaft was lighter though, a pretty candy bar–brown. I opened up for his entrance. He slid it along my tongue into my mouth. I continued jacking my own dick as I feasted on his. Mike D grabbed the back of my head, forcing it down his shaft. "You like that shit, huh? Fuck yeah!" He had these big, low-hanging balls. I wanted to take them in my mouth like jawbreakers, but time was against us. Mike D began to pivot faster. I tried like hell to keep up. "You know you want this nut." Mike D held my head down until he shot cum down my gullet. I gagged a little, but took what he had to give.

I felt myself getting close, dick hard and spit-sloppy. I came in the time it took for Mike D to blink his pretty brown eyes. His essence seeped over my fingers. Mike D pushed his wet dick back into his shorts and quietly exited Brandon's room. Just in time, too. Brandon was done showering. I grabbed Brandon's shirt to wipe up my mess. I slid off his bed and started to get dressed. I felt like I had been fucked with an elephant's dick. Brandon walked out with a towel wrapped around his slim waist.

"Damn, what time is it?" I asked.

"A lil' bit after three." Brandon barely gave me eye contact as he retrieved the empty beer bottles off the floor.

He opened his dresser drawer, plucked out a pair of clean boxers, and put them on under the towel. I asked him if he wanted my number.

"I don't know, man. I'm always catching Janiece going through my phone. Send me a message on Facebook. I'm under Brandon M." He ushered me out of the room into the hall like I was some cheap crack ho. "I'll get you and your boys some passes."

"Remember: live to work, don't work to live, brotha."

I descended down the stairs and out of the house. Mike D was sitting on the stoop smoking a Black 'n' Mild like he had just gotten the blow job of the century.

"Nice meeting you," was all I said.

"Don't forget them passes."

"I'll come by on Thursday and drop 'em off," I said.

"Come check me out. I'll be around."

"That's wa'ssup."

"See ya soon, new booty." I got in my car and drove off anticipating my next visit to the historic black frat house.

ABOUT THE AUTHORS

RICK ARCHER is an up-and-coming writer in the erotica world. He currently lives in New York and can be contacted at writerguy12@gmail.com.

GAVIN ATLAS attended George Washington University where he performed as a disc jockey at fraternity parties. Among other works, he is the author of the erotic short-story collection, *The Boy Can't Help It*. He lives in Houston with his boyfriend, John. Gavin can be reached at GavinAtlas.com.

RACHEL KRAMER BUSSEL (rachelkramerbussel.com) is a New York–based author, editor and blogger. She is senior editor at *Penthouse Variations*. Her books include *Crossdressing, The Mile High Club, Bottoms Up, Spanked, Peep Show, Tasting Him, Do Not Disturb* and more.

LANDON DIXON's writing credits include *Men, Freshmen, Mandate, Torso, Honcho, Bear,* and stories in the anthologies *Working Stiff, Sex by the Book, Boys Caught In the Act, Service with a Smile, Nerdvana, Homo Thugs, Black Fire, Ultimate Gay Erotica 2005, 2007,* and *2008,* and *Best Gay Erotica 2009.*

HANK EDWARDS's humorous erotic novels, *Fluffers, Inc.* and *A Carnal Cruise* are available from Lethe Press. His erotic romance novel *Destiny's Bastard* and erotic suspense novella, *Holed Up* are available from Loose Id in e-book format. Visit his website at www.hankedwardsbooks.com.

Z. FERGUSON is a writer living in Seattle who has written for Xcite, Cleansheets, Good Vibrations and the former Ruthie's Club. He writes both straight and gay erotica and is currently working on a collection of shorts entitled, *Adventures in Vanilla.*

JEFF FUNK's stories have appeared in *Hard Working Men, Skater Boys, Cruise Lines, Hard Hats, My First Time Vol. 5, Ultimate Gay Erotica 2008, Tales of Travelrotica for Gay Men Vol. 2* and *Dorm Porn 2.* He lives in Auburn, Indiana.

KYLE LUKOFF is a writer and student living in Brooklyn, New York. He has been previously published in a wide variety of anthologies including *I Like It Like That: True Stories of Gay Male Desire* and *Men At Noon, Monsters At Midnight.*

JEFF MANN has published two books of poetry, *Bones Washed with Wine* and *On the Tongue*; a collection of memoir and poetry, *Loving Mountains, Loving Men*; a book of essays, *Edge*; and a volume of short fiction, *A History of Barbed Wire,* winner of a Lambda Literary Award.

BOB MASTERS has had work appear in the *James White Review* and *RFD*. He is currently working on his first novel.

GREGORY L. NORRIS is a full-time professional writer with work routinely published in national magazines and fiction anthologies and is the author of the handbook to all-things-Sunnydale, *The Q Guide to Buffy the Vampire Slayer*. Norris lives at and writes from the outer limits of New Hampshire.

CHRISTOPHER PIERCE is the editor of *I Like to Watch* and *Biker Boys* (Cleis Press) and the author of *Kidnapped by a Sex Maniac: The Erotic Fiction of Christopher Pierce*. His fiction has appeared in many publications. Visit him online at christopherpierceerotica.com.

NEIL PLAKCY is a prolific author of gay mystery, romance and erotica. He went to college in Philadelphia, and wishes there had been a branch of Lambda Lambda Lambda there when he was a student. Find out more about him and his books at www.mahubooks.com.

ROB ROSEN, author of *Sparkle: The Queerest Book You'll Ever Love* and *Divas Las Vegas*, has contributed to the Cleis Press collections: *Truckers, Best Gay Romance, Hard Hats, Backdraft, Surfer Boys, Bears, Special Forces, College Boys, Biker Boys, Hard Working Men, Afternoon Pleasures* and *Gay Quickies*. Please visit him at therobrosen.com

Residing on English Bay in Vancouver, Canada, **JAY STARRE** has fiction appearing in *Best Gay Romance 2008, Best Gay Bondage, Bears, Surfer Boys , Special Forces* and *Skater Boys*. He is the author of two historical gay novels, *The Erotic Tales of* *the Knights Templars* and *The Lusty Adventures of the Knossos Prince.*

After moving several times about the country and Europe, **C. C. WILLIAMS** currently resides in the Southwestern United States with his partner JT. When not critiquing cooking or dancing contestants on TV, he is at work on several writing projects. He invites you to find out more at ccwilliamsonline.net.

ABOUT
THE EDITOR

SHANE ALLISON is the proud editor of *Hot Cops: Gay Erotic Stories, Backdraft: Fireman Erotica, Hard Working Men: Gay Erotic Stories, Afternoon Pleasures: Erotica for Gay Couples, Brief Encounters: 69 Gay Erotic Shorts* and *College Boys: Gay Erotic Stories* (winner of the 2011 TLA Gaybie Award for Gay Erotic Fiction). His stories have appeared in *Best Black Gay Erotica*, five editions of *Best Gay Erotica, Bears, Biker Boys, Leathermen, Surfer Boys, Country Boys* and over a dozen other lusty anthologies. His first book of poems, *Slut Machine* is out from Rebel Satori Press. Shane is single and currently living in Tallahassee, Florida.

More Gay Erotic Stories from Shane Allison

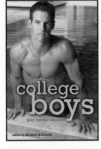

College Boys
Gay Erotic Stories
Edited by Shane Allison

First feelings of lust for another boy, all-night study
sessions, the excitement of a student hot for a teacher...
is it any wonder that college boys are the objects of
fantasy the world over?
ISBN 978-1-57344-399-9 $14.95

Hot Cops
Gay Erotic Stories
Edited by Shane Allison

"From smooth and fit to big and hairy...
it's like a downtown locker room where
everyone has some sort of badge."—*Bay
Area Reporter*
ISBN 978-1-57344-277-0 $14.95

Backdraft
Fireman Erotica
Edited by Shane Allison

"Seriously: This book is so scorching hot
that you should box it with a fire extin-
guisher and ointment. It will burn more
than your fingers." —*Tucson Weekly*
ISBN 978-1-57344-325-8 $14.95

More of the Very Best from Cleis Press

Best Gay Erotica 2010
Edited by Richard Labonté
Selected and introduced by Blair Mastbaum
ISBN 978-1-57344-374-6 $15.95

Skater Boys
Gay Erotic Stories
Edited by Neil Plakcy
ISBN 978-1-57344-401-9 $14.95

Best of the Best Gay Erotica 3
Edited by Richard Labonté
ISBN 978-1-57344-410-1 $14.95

A Sticky End
A Mitch Mitchell Mystery
By James Lear
ISBN 978-1-57344-395-1 $14.95

Ordering is easy! Call us toll free or fax us to place your MC/VISA order.
You can also mail the order form below with payment to:
Cleis Press, 2246 Sixth St., Berkeley, CA 94710.

Buy 4 books,
Get 1 *FREE**

ORDER FORM

QTY	TITLE	PRICE
____	_____	_____
____	_____	_____
____	_____	_____
____	_____	_____
____	_____	_____
____	_____	_____
____	_____	_____

	SUBTOTAL	_____
	SHIPPING	_____
	SALES TAX	_____
	TOTAL	_____

Add $3.95 postage/handling for the first book ordered and $1.00 for each additional
book. Outside North America, please contact us for shipping rates. California residents
add 8.75% sales tax. Payment in U.S. dollars only.

* Free book of equal or lesser value. Shipping and applicable sales tax extra.

Cleis Press • Phone: (800) 780-2279 • Fax: (510) 845-8001
orders@cleispress.com • www.cleispress.com
You'll find more great books on our website

Follow us on Twitter @cleispress • Friend/fan us on Facebook